Book Three of The Edenville Series

Danielle Stewart

Copyright Page

An *Original* work of Danielle Stewart.
Stars in a Bottle Copyright 2015 by Danielle Stewart

ISBN-13: 978-1514152379
ISBN-10: 1514152371

Cover Design by Ginny Gallagher
(http://ginsbooknotes.com)

Note to the Reader

The Native American Reservation and people mentioned in this book is a work of fiction. I was lucky enough to spend time out in the region and learn more about some of the topics and issues covered in Stars in a Bottle. I was shocked to hear of some of the challenges that still exist today for people living on reservations and I hope that changes continue to be made to help improve some of the circumstances.

Dedication

Every stage of life has its own challenges. I don't think it's any easier to be a teenager than it is to try to raise one. This book is dedicated to my parents for surviving three rounds of raising teenage girls. We didn't make it easy but somehow we all made it through. Thank you!

Also this book is dedicated to my son Jack. We have years to go before you are a teenager but please always remember you can come home. No matter what is going on in your world we are here for you.

Synopsis

Frankie Cooper has grown up surrounded by her outrageous family in the small town of Edenville, North Carolina. The problem with growing up with a suffocating family is that even though her eighteenth birthday is behind her they still don't see her as an adult.

But when she's finally in the arms of the man she's been dreaming about, none of that matters.
She's been in love with Maxwell for years and nothing will get in the way starting her life with him. She only needs to prove to her family that she's capable and then they'll learn to let her go.

Will she finally convince her family she's ready to be on her own or will she come crashing back to reality and realize she's thrown a match on the bridge that should lead her back home?

Prologue

Frankie

Admitting I'm wrong is not an option. If I let loose the waterfall of nagging worry about my choice to jump a train all alone, it would be like confessing I've screwed up. So instead I crank up the volume on my music until I'm sure the woman next to me can hear the thumping through my headphones. I remind myself that fear never did anything to change the world. It only slows the process.

Even with the music rattling in my ears I keep imagining the scene unfolding back in Edenville. My grandmother Betty will have found my note by now. She'll have called my mother and the entire family has probably snapped into action. My police officer uncle Bobby is undoubtedly trying unsuccessfully to track my cell phone I turned off and pulled the battery from. My father will be barking at a bank teller to release information about the joint account he and I share. But there will be no clues there either; I moved most of the money to a new account last week. One he doesn't have access to. Their heads will be spinning with worry and anger, and every second will be torture. *For that I am sorry.*

The real problem is turning eighteen didn't magically make them see me as an adult. They didn't throw a party to welcome me to the club of grown-ups. They still picture me as the freckle-faced little girl who they need to shield from the world. But I've always felt ready to fly. I've just been waiting for them to open my cage and set me free into the world.

My family will have to deal with that. They'll have to find a way to understand I am not meant to spend my life in Edenville, or maybe not even North Carolina. The world is big and broken, and I want to see it without the cheery sanitized view through the filter my parents have provided. There is more waiting for me than quiet nights on my grandmother's porch. There has to be.

As trees rush by and the landscape around me changes from everything I've grown up watching to something I've never seen before, I can feel my courage finally outweighing my fear. I can do this. I have to ignore what my parents are afraid I can't do and remember what they've shown me I am capable of doing.

Chapter One

"You ever been on a train before?" the crinkle-faced old woman beside Frankie asked as she offered her a handful of saltines.

Frankie politely declined the crackers and put into action all the tidbits of advice her father had ever given her. Don't take food from a stranger. Don't look as though you don't belong or are vulnerable in any scenario. Come across as confident. "I've done this trip a few times," Frankie lied, casually shrugging her off.

"Wow, you seem so young. How far are you going on this line? I'm heading to Tennessee. My grandkids are there, and I go twice a year to see them. Can't count on my son and my grouchy daughter-in-law to ever bring the kids to me."

Frankie nodded her head as though she could relate when clearly she couldn't. "I'm getting off in Arkansas," she lied again. No one needed to know her destination, or at least that was the advice ringing in her mind from her father, Michael. He'd always been her traveling buddy. High school, for an active student like Frankie, meant opportunities to see the country. There were school trips for the top students and conventions and rallies around topics she was passionate about. Her mother, Jules, was usually tied up tending to her brother, Ian, and not as comfortable traveling as her father. So when the time came to hear a speech at the nation's capital or receive a certificate for a job well done in Charlotte, Frankie and Michael would pack their bags and head off. It was strange not having him beside her. Strange but exciting.

Every trip they'd taken was like a crash course in the do's and don'ts of travel. Make sure you have a good understanding of the area you'll be going to. Make sure you are aware of your surroundings and not lost in some media or distraction. Don't tell people your business just because they ask. Don't pack heavy. Have cash in case of an emergency. But don't flash it around when you go to pay for something. Every one of these rules was blazed into her mind as she stared out the window and put her headphones back on.

She looked down at her watch and realized that was pointless. When you had twenty-six hours on a train you didn't need to check the time every fifteen minutes. The best thing she could do was sleep. Closing her eyes, she tried to picture the adventure ahead rather than the wake of trouble she'd caused by leaving.

The first image in her mind was the face she spent hours a day dreaming about. Maxwell Clement was everything Frankie had ever wanted in a guy, even before she'd realized it. They'd met four years ago when Frankie and her father had gone to a university in West Virginia for her debate club championships, and there, on the other side of the stage, ready to debate her, was Maxwell.

She was first drawn in by his hair: like cleanly cut spun silk, it was glowing under the stage lights, almost white rather than blond. When she strained to get a better look, she was taken in by his perfection. He was much taller than any other student on the stage, but he held his height well. He didn't stoop under the weight of insecurity; instead his back was arrow straight with long-practiced good posture. Somehow his skin had managed to evade the acne that plagued most kids readying for the debate. Everything about him seemed flawlessly sculpted and groomed, from his blue school blazer right down to his argyle socks.

When the group was announced before the debate began, Frankie discovered Maxwell was a senior. She was a freshman but such a dynamite debater she'd been recruited to lead the team. But she had proved her recruiters wrong during that debate. The age gap between Maxwell and her was why everyone had assumed he would crush her when they each took a side on the topic of raising minimum wage in the United States. People figured her sweaty hands and dry stuttering mouth were from the nerves of speaking in front of a large crowd at such a young age. But in fact, Maxwell's shining blond hair and perfect skin had kept her from making any valid points. She had been close enough to him now to see his hazel eyes and wide dimpled smile. He had bowled her over in a way she'd never experienced before.

But the spell didn't last long. After the debate she had been so angry with herself she marched up to Maxwell to argue her very valid points on minimum wage. She'd stepped in his way as he'd headed to a group of his peers and had begun reciting everything she'd been unable to state while on stage. When he'd tried to cut in and counter, she'd spoken quickly and concisely to stop him. Her awe of him on the stage had reflected back in his own impressed eyes. Their connection to each other had been instant and impossible to ignore.

From that point on they'd kept in touch. It started slow. Just the occasional email regarding topics they might both find interesting. But every time his name popped up on her email she felt butterflies take flight in her stomach. For the first time in her life she'd found something that could distract her from her normal laser-beam focus.

She and Maxwell had seen each other a few more times on the debate circuit before he graduated that year. The thought that he'd be going off to college had broken her heart. He wasn't hers; it wasn't as if they were dating. Certainly not in a traditional way. But he held her heart in his hand, and that meant he could crush it at any moment. She could just picture the college girls, women really, who'd be throwing themselves at a guy like him. But if there were droves of them, he was gentleman enough never to bring it up. More than that, he continued to stay in touch with Frankie when she was sure it would have been easier to just forget she existed. Their little jokes were still funny. The world hadn't ended with him going to college in Boston. Frankie's delicate heart was still in one piece.

The highlights of their relationship had been the two times Maxwell had come to Edenville for a visit. The first time he had stayed with Frankie's Uncle Bobby and Aunt Piper while attending a college chess tournament in Raleigh. The second trip had been the turning point for them. She had just celebrated her sweet sixteen and he brought her a beautiful charm bracelet. While they sat out by the creek, Maxwell relentlessly quizzed Frankie on SAT questions, like a warrior attacking a strong fortress. It was what she liked about him. He knew how smart Frankie was, and instead of just pandering to it, he challenged her. That's when the bet happened. For every right answer she would earn a kiss from him. Her body went rigid, frozen by the idea that what she had always hoped for was about to happen.

That was a bet she had been determined to win. And she had. After ten little kisses had come one long one she was sure to remember for the rest of her life. It was then and there he'd told her how he felt about her. He'd confessed that no other girl he'd met or dated could compare to Frankie. She was all he'd ever wanted. That had been the moment all her daydreams had crashed together and had woven into reality.

A crush can be a very aptly named thing. If the love is not reciprocated then you most certainly are crushed. But when you hear the person you've been dreaming about, pining over, and secretly planning your future with, admit that he feels the same way, it's like strapping yourself to a rocket and heading for outer space. There had been just one problem, and his name was Dad.

Everyone liked Maxwell. Her whole family had called him a good guy with a bright future. But the age gap had made anything besides friendship impossible. Her father, though actually very fond of Maxwell, had laid down the law early. Frankie was only sixteen and Maxwell nineteen, on the verge of turning twenty. It wasn't going to happen. End of story.

Knowing this, Maxwell had told Frankie that the kiss would be the only one they'd share for now. He wouldn't lie to her father and sneak around. But he would be patient. He would talk to her on the phone every chance he had, and they would plan a future together. But not without her father's blessing. It had seemed like something impossible to maintain, but somehow they'd made it work. They video-chatted a few times a week and exchanged in-depth emails that would probably be the equivalent of love letters in her grandparents' day.

As she stared out the train's window and thought of her parents, she knew they'd see her actions as running away to be with a boy. She hated the idea of that. It made her sound immature and fickle. That wasn't the reason she was on this journey. It was for them really. She wanted them to see what she was capable of. She needed them to get used of the idea of her being on her own. There was a promising story she wanted to investigate in Arizona, and it would be enough to prove to them she was more than just a kid. And with Maxwell by her side, she knew she could do anything.

Conveniently and not entirely coincidently, Maxwell was about to start law school in Arizona. Her best friend Shayna, who'd given her the idea to research this issue, lived on a Native American reservation a couple hours from the university. This was going to be the trip of her life. She'd be able to visit her friend, finally be able to connect on a real level with Maxwell, and put her name on an article that might gain some attention. Everything had fallen into place.

For as long as Frankie could remember, her dream was to be a journalist. The kind who broke stories no one else was paying attention to. Until they'd read her article and then everyone would be talking about it. Together she and Maxwell would be an unstoppable team, and it would start with this one lead. They'd unite behind a story she was sure would garner attention and take her career down the right path. It would show her parents she had the necessary skills. They'd have no choice but to take her seriously. In the fall they'd be ready for the big change. They'd still be angry about her decision to give up her scholarship in North Carolina and move to Arizona to go to school with Maxwell. But they'd just have to deal with it. That is, once she worked up the guts to tell them; they'd have to deal with it.

But that was down the road. For now it was only about this trip. Twenty-one hours to go. Less than a day and she'd be putting the soles of her shoes down in a place she'd never been before with no chaperone to tell her what to do. Or more importantly, *what not to do*. She'd be investigating something that mattered. And she'd be doing so with the guy she'd pined after for the last four years. That was all going to have to be enough to get her to digest the lump of guilt currently choking her.

Chapter Two

There was no freshening up after the long train ride. It was unfortunate to have to see Maxwell with her mascara smudged and her red hair pulled back into a ponytail. She wanted to look her best whenever she had a chance to be with him. Even before a video chat she'd spend all her time trying to look flawless. As she glanced into the small compact mirror from her makeup bag, she groaned. It had been a gift from her grandmother. And worse than that, the eyes looking back at her were those of her mother, making it hard to try to forget what must be happening in Edenville right now.

Snapping the compact closed, she slung her bag over her shoulder and shimmied her way past the man sleeping in the seat next to her. If everything was going according to plan, Maxwell would be waiting for her in front of the train station, ready to take her to dinner and then back to his hotel. She understood the implications of the enormous step that meant for the two of them. But she was ready. She had waited long enough, had appeased her parents. It was her time now. That's what she chanted in her mind as she hopped off the train.

When the bustling crowd broke away she stood alone on the sidewalk for a moment in the hot desert air. She'd never experienced this arid warmth before. The humidity back in North Carolina was enough to perm your hair most days. But it was many degrees hotter here, and while people tried to downplay what it was like, she felt like the rubber of her shoes would melt to the pavement if she didn't move to the shade. But she loved it.

As she pulled in a deep breath of air, she saw him. Maxwell was jogging toward her with a solemn gaze. They'd called him. They'd gotten hold of him, and he knew the truth now. A setback, but she knew she could explain now they were face to face.

"Seriously, Frankie?" he asked, pulling her in for a hug. Jax #7. That was the cologne he wore, and it was enough to send chills up her spine every time she smelled it. Other guys she knew wore it but none had the exact mixture of his skin and the musky scent. There were times she'd purposefully forgotten to dress warmly enough so she could borrow his college sweatshirt. They'd spent so little time in person she had to take advantage of those situations when they came up.

After wearing it an entire afternoon around Edenville the smell would have thoroughly infiltrated her hair and skin. Even after handing the shirt back it was as if he was still there with her. That was what it meant to be in love she thought.

"Your dad was blowing up my phone. How could you not tell them you were leaving? How could you not tell them where you were going? They don't want you out here alone." Maxwell stepped back and looked down at her disappointedly.

"I'm an adult," Frankie shot back, trying to temper her attitude. "I don't need to check in with them for everything I do. Plus, I'm not alone. You're here." She meant that to sound like an adult and maybe a little flirtatious. But he didn't flush, actually quite the opposite. All the blood drained from his cheeks as he pulled her toward the bench and sat her down.

"Your father is furious. It's a damn good thing I didn't go into more detail about why you were coming

11

here. I'm guessing they know nothing about our apartment, about you no longer going to school in North Carolina, or any of our plans. How could you put me in that position?" he asked so seriously that it took out all the excitement for Frankie.

"You don't understand what they're like," Frankie explained. "I'm eighteen. I can go where I want, when I want. You and I have been waiting for this for a long time. I thought you'd be excited. I left them a note."

"A note?" Maxwell coughed out. "You left them a note that you were getting on a train and going to Arizona? They must be going out of their minds. Have they called you?"

"No," Frankie answered, feeling like she was being scolded. "Well they may have. I'm not sure. I've had my phone off. I didn't want them coming after me. You know how they are."

"Yes, I know exactly how they are, and I know they care about you very much. I can't believe you would just run off like that and not give them a way to contact you. That's very selfish, Frankie. I promised your dad the second I saw you I'd have you call." Maxwell pulled his cell phone from his pocket and shoved it toward her.

"Does no one understand I am an adult? I don't need permission to go anywhere. I certainly don't need you and my father deciding what I have to do." She stared down at his cell phone as though he was handing her a fresh pile of hot garbage.

"It's not about permission, Frankie. Being an adult means being confident enough in your own choices not to have to sneak around and hurt other people. Grown-ups don't leave notes." He pushed the cell phone closer to her with an insistent look on his face.

To say she was crushed would be an understatement. All she wanted was for Maxwell to see her as an equal, but what she thought would do that had actually pushed her further in the other direction.

He looked down at her again with a stern glare. "If you don't call them, I will. I like your family a lot, and I hope they like me, too. I'm not going to jeopardize my relationship with them over this. I don't want them to think I had anything to do with the way this went down."

"I'm staying out here," Frankie insisted. "I'll call them and tell them where I am and that I'm safe, but I'm not going back home. I believe in what we're out here to do. Don't you? It's going to be big." She needed this from him. Even when they seemed to be on completely different levels, her talking about junior prom and him talking college fraternities, they could always find common causes. They were equally passionate about so many things, justice being one thread they were always sewn together with.

"Of course I do. Together, you and I are a powerhouse. I'm as anxious as you are to see it through. I assumed you'd told your family about all our plans. Not just this trip but our future. We can talk about that over dinner. You just check in with your family, please. They're worried."

His phone rang, playing some song as it sat in his palm, and she snatched it away. She knew well enough who it was.

"Hello," she said, letting the annoyance show through.

"Frankie?" her father asked, sounding relieved. HIs relief was quickly replaced with anger. "She's there. She's with Maxwell." She heard her father explain to everyone who must have been circled around him. There was a rustling on the phone before her mother came on.

"Frankie honey, tell me exactly where you are," Jules said in a forced flat tone that actually worried Frankie more than if she were shouting.

"Why aren't you yelling?" Frankie asked, holding the phone away from her ear slightly in case it was about to start.

"Because your grandmother told me if I yell at you and you hang up before I get a chance to find anything out she'd kill me. And if I'm dead I won't be around to kill you for running away."

Frankie rolled her eyes at her mother's words. "It's not running away when you're eighteen. I knew you would do everything possible to keep me from coming if you heard, so I thought it would be easier on all of us if I just went."

"Easier on us?" her father called out.

"Listen," Frankie said curtly, "I'm in Arizona. Maxwell and I have been following a story for a while. Shayna tipped us off about it. We were researching it and came across some things I think could make a great article. I came out to put it all together. It's no big deal." Frankie could feel Maxwell's disapproving eyes on her as she tried to casually explain away how it all had happened.

"No big deal?" Jules scoffed. "You run off to the other side of the country with a boy, and you want to say it's no big deal. You know I really liked Maxwell, but I expected more out of him. I guess we know better now. Things will certainly be changing around here."

"I'm glad I won't be there to see the changes then," Frankie shot back, knowingly tossing gasoline on the fire of her family.

"Child," Betty crowed then quieted and gave way to Jules's much louder interjection.

"You better watch your manners, little girl. At least we were happy to hear Maxwell didn't know about this ridiculous note scheme. He was wrong to think you were ready to go out there by yourself, but at least he knew better than to be sneaky about it."

"I guess I'm the only dumb one who was under the impression I was old enough to make my own decisions. I am eighteen." She felt like a broken record having to repeat her age to everyone who kept treating her like a child.

The rustling on the phone again indicated someone else was coming to hover over the speaker and weigh in. Her grandmother's voice was high and angry as she started in on her. "You've been eighteen for about a second," she scolded. "The wax on your birthday candles is still hot. You might not be aware of this but you look as though you still need your crust cut off your sandwiches, and right now you're acting like it, too. Leaving like that is not a grown-up thing to do, it's about as childish as it gets."

"That's what Maxwell said," Frankie admitted as she finally looked up and met his eyes. They'd softened now as he watched her take her lumps from her worried family.

"Then you've got two smart people you should start listening to. I promised your mother once I knew you were alive I'd butt out. But child, I swear on my Bible, if you ever give me a scare like that again I will never cook you another meal in your life." She'd thrown down the ultimate punishment that said she meant business, and Frankie could hear her mumbling more angry threats as she walked away from the phone.

"I'm sorry, Mom," Frankie said quietly. "I didn't want to deal with all the drama of me leaving, so I just bailed, and I know that must have been scary. I'll turn my phone back on."

Jules let out a long sigh and sounded like she was on the verge of tears. "We can talk about it more when you get home. Your father and I can wire some money for the ticket back. Are you still at the train station? Can you see when the next ticket is available? We can stay on the phone while you check."

Frankie scoffed at that idea. "I'm not coming back right now, Mom. I'm going do to what I came out here to do; Shayna is going to work out interviews for me at her reservation. I've got money for a ticket back when that time comes."

"You are not staying out there with Maxwell and parading around doing who knows what. Get your butt back on that train or—" Jules caught her breath as she paused to think through the consequences.

"Or what?" Frankie asked, feeling fairly confident. "I have plenty of money saved up. I've been working at the restaurant since I was twelve. I worked my ass off for scholarships to pay for college. You can't ground me. You can't cut me off financially. So you can't make me come home."

The silence on the other end of the line didn't feel quite as victorious as Frankie had imagined. Beating her parents in an argument had rarely happened, but this felt different than any others before. She'd practiced this speech, but actually saying the words out loud made her feel sick.

"Frankie," Jules whispered, "please don't do this. You aren't ready to be out there on your own. There is so much that can happen. There is so much you just aren't prepared for." Her voice was pleading now and it tugged at Frankie's heart, but she stayed the course.

"Mom, in three months I'm leaving for college. We're talking frat guys and keg parties and making sure no one slipped anything into my drink. Do you want to hear the stats for how dangerous it is for a girl to live on a college campus? But you and Dad have already prepared me for all of this stuff. What does Grammy always say? You don't build the bridge over troubled water for your kids; you give them the lumber. Life is about to start for me one way or another. I just want some say in it."

"But this summer," Jules croaked. "I thought we'd have this time before you go. There was so much more I wanted to do with you. We'd shop for all your dorm room stuff and spend as much time as possible together. I'm not ready yet." Like a dagger to the heart, Frankie could hear her mother's choked-back tears finally falling.

"Mom," Frankie swallowed hard, "please don't be sad. I thought you'd be mad; I was prepared for angry, but sad I can't deal with. I won't be out here that long. I'll be back to do all that stuff. I just need a little time, that's all."

"Fine," her father's voice boomed. "Tell me right now whether or not you agree with this statement. *We are still your parents and that matters.* Maybe you don't need our money and our permission, but that doesn't mean you're never going to need us again. Agree?"

There were times Frankie loved her father's matter of fact, cut to the chase approach. But right now was not one of them. He had her cornered. She knew damn well at some point in her life she'd need her parents again. "Agree," Frankie offered back to her father.

"Then there will be terms to your staying out there." Her father's voice was chopped short by her mother's interjecting.

"Are you kidding me, Michael? Our daughter is across the country alone with a boy. No, not a boy, a man. Maxwell is twenty-one years old. You're going to make a plea deal with her? This is not some trial; it's our child." The phone went instantly silent, and Frankie pulled it away from her ear to make sure they hadn't disconnected. She knew instead someone had hit the mute button while the group on the other end collectively debated her fate.

"I want to know what you're doing out there," Michael's voice cut back in sharply. "Don't give me the sanitized version either. If there is something besides Maxwell that drew you in Arizona it has to be good enough to have your attention. I want to know what it is."

Frankie hadn't planned this much explanation. She'd told herself over and over that when push came to shove she'd just keep reminding them she was an adult. But her father had played the very strategic card of having her agree that she was still *their child,* and that meant something. "Seventeen years ago a young woman from the Tewapia Indian tribe disappeared. Her boyfriend at the time, a white man from a town neighboring the reservation, was accused of murdering her. No body was ever found, but when they searched his apartment they discovered he'd attempted to clean up a large amount of blood. Through DNA they determined it was that of the missing girl. But the reservation does not have it's own media outlet so the only coverage of the crime was in the papers off the reservation. There was a total of four pieces written about it. They covered the spree of mailboxes being vandalized more thoroughly than they did this murder. I'm using that case to cite a very large journalistic bias for crimes that take place on the reservation."

"And who are you going to push this piece to? Obviously the local papers won't cover it," Michael added and she loved how sharp her father was on these things.

"No, of course not, but I've got a contact at this watch-dog group who polices things like this. They help bring attention to heavily slanted media outlets that don't report the full story or, even worse, flat-out lie."

"Did these papers lie?"

"There might be an element of conspiracy actually. The day the warrant went out for the boyfriend he reportedly died in a car accident. The papers widely covered the accident and made sure to give it front-page space, as if they were trying to close the book on it. I think there is a chance the boyfriend didn't die at all."

"It's awfully convenient," Michael retorted.

"Exactly." Frankie knew her father well. He could never resist a good mystery. He had a penchant for spotting holes in a story. They'd spent plenty of late hours poring over old cases of his, looking for missed opportunities. "There is an enormous tension between the reservation and the surrounding areas. You know the reservations have their own constitutions and are policed by the Bureau of Indian Affairs. There were always problems between the local police and people of the reservation, but this was a tipping point. Danyia, the murdered girl, was the daughter of one of the high-ranking leaders of the tribe, and everything began to fall apart. Even to this day the damage hasn't been repaired. The contact I have will publish this article, and it could get some mainstream attention. It's an untapped topic. They've never dealt with Native American territories because they've never had a contact. With Shayna helping me, I could get a really fresh angle."

"So you're going to tell that story and try to repair the damage?" her mother asked hopefully. Frankie could almost hear the words that weren't being said. *That's not so bad. How much trouble can you get into doing that?*

"No," Michael answered before Frankie could. "That wouldn't be enough to get her out there. There has to be something more dangerous than that."

"It's not dangerous, Dad. We found multiple cases of inaccurate information and downright lies being published. It could be a great scoop."

"And if the conspiracy goes deeper than you think, like the police department or the public officials, you still believe it won't be risky?" Michael's tone was flat but Frankie knew this was a leading question.

"I have no intention of finding out how deep it goes," Frankie lied. "I'm going to start the dialogue on the story by writing an article and hopefully sparking an investigation. That's all."

"Likely story," her father scoffed. "So when you fall down this rabbit hole and find yourself in a jam, what are you going to do?"

"Dad," Frankie huffed, but he cut her off.

"Because, as much as I want you to know how mad and disappointed we are, I don't want you to think you can't count on us if you get in a jam. If you call, we'll come."

Frankie felt a lump in her throat, too big to swallow back. It took her a long moment to blink away the tears and croak out an answer. "I know, Daddy. I know you'll come if I needed you."

"You will check in every day. And not with the same person. You have to talk to someone new in this family. No calling just your Aunt Piper or Grandpa Clay. Rotate through all of us."

"Why?" Frankie asked. "Can't I just call one of you to spread the word?"

"Everyone in this family knows you differently. I want to make sure we all have a chance to hear your voice every couple days so we can compare notes. Call every day, talk to one of us. Are we clear?"

"Yes, Dad," Frankie groaned.

"Now let me talk to Maxwell." Michael's voice was noticeably deeper and suddenly more assertive than usual.

"Why?" Frankie shot back nervously.

"Because there are conditions for him as well. Now put him on the phone, and not speakerphone either."

She was compelled to beg him not to do this, but she knew it would fall on deaf ears. Having a protective family was a blessing in so many situations, but when it came to boyfriends it had proven very awkward. Turning her eyes up at Maxwell apologetically, she stretched the phone out for him to take.

Because Maxwell was a good sport and a man with integrity, he took the phone with only a breath of hesitation. Frankie's palms instantly began to sweat as she heard Maxwell stutter.

"Yes, Michael, sir . . . I mean, of course." His face was blazing like a tourist's sunburn, and his eyes darted from left to right. She could only imagine what her father was saying on the other end of the line. "I do know what you're capable of sir. I completely understand where you're coming from. You need me to say what words?" Maxwell asked, swallowing hard. "Oh yes, I swear on my life."

Frankie buried her face in her hands and wished she could disappear behind them forever.

When it was finally over the call disconnected, the bustling crowd of the train station seemed to hit a lull, and Frankie felt her knees grow weak. "I'm so sorry," was all she could think to say.

"Let's just go to dinner. We can talk about it then. You must be hungry."

She could only muster a little nod as she placed her bag in Maxwell's waiting hand. As they headed for his car, Frankie took a few deep breaths and let a swell of excitement wash away the prickly tension of all that had transpired. Because even though people were plenty mad at her and everything felt upside down, she was about to sit down across from the guy who held her heart and eat dinner without one of her parents cutting into the conversation every two seconds. It would just be the two of them, finally getting a chance to experience each other with no filters. That's all she'd ever wanted. He's all she'd ever wanted.

Chapter Three

"This place is beautiful. I'm a mess. I wish we could have gone back to the hotel to change first." Frankie took the cloth napkin from the table, unfolded it, and placed it across her lap. The thin-lipped, nose-in-the-air waiter came by with a bottle of sparkling water in a bucket of ice and began silently filling their glasses.

"You look beautiful," Maxwell insisted with his soft smile. "You don't have to be all dressed up to be gorgeous."

"Thank you," Frankie said with a blush, turning her eyes away from the waiter. She'd felt closer to Maxwell than anyone in her life even though most of their time was spent physically apart. She knew she loved him and he loved her. They respected her parents' wishes, but that didn't keep them from connecting on a level seeming to link their very souls.

Maxwell nodded his head in gratitude to the waiter. "Can we see the wine list too please?"

"Absolutely, sir," the waiter retorted. "I'll need to see your driver's licenses to verify your ages."

Like a shot to the heart Frankie felt herself turn from a blush to a full-on blaze, her skin likely so red her freckles were camouflaged. "I left mine out in the car," Frankie announced with a crack in her voice. "But you still get some, Maxwell. Don't skip it on my account."

Maxwell dug his wallet out of his pocket and flashed the waiter what he needed to see, sending the man off for a wine list.

"I'm so sorry," Frankie groaned covering her hot face. "I hate that."

Danielle Stewart

"You're sorry you're not old enough to drink?" Maxwell asked, shrugging it off. "It's no big deal."

"But you're mad about something," Frankie noted tentatively, reading the weird flashes in his eyes. "You can't take what my dad said personally. It doesn't matter anyway. We're out here, and they're back there, and we just have to put it out of our minds and enjoy each other."

"No," Maxwell said, hanging his head as though the disappointment was too heavy to lift. "We can't put it out of our minds. We have to talk about it."

"I don't see the point. They aren't ruling my life. We finally have our chance to be together on our own and really start our relationship. I thought you'd be happier about that."

"I would be if that was about to happen," Maxwell cut back, his voice nipping with anger. "We aren't going to have a chance to be together the way we planned this trip."

"Why not?" Frankie asked, her elbow accidently knocking her knife into her plate and sending a loud clinking noise through the restaurant.

"Because I just made a commitment to your father that I would not take advantage of this situation. I promised him I would treat you the same way I would if he was here. I promised him nothing would happen between us that wouldn't happen if he were on this trip." The anger was ever present in his voice but she appreciated he was trying to wrangle it.

"You know damn well you aren't taking advantage of anything. I am here because I want to be. Anything we do while I'm here is my choice. To insinuate anything else is insulting and pretty much saying I don't have enough sense in my head to make my own choices."

24

"Frankie, it doesn't matter. It doesn't matter if your father was right or wrong. I made a commitment to him, and I'm not going to break it. We have to readjust our plans for this trip, and we need to talk about how exactly we're going forward."

"What is that supposed to mean?" Frankie asked, tears springing up shockingly fast though she managed to keep them from falling. Losing Maxwell was not an option. She wouldn't allow it.

"You haven't told them you are coming out here for school in the fall? They still think you're going to college back in North Carolina. They don't realize you and I have a future planned. Why wouldn't they be worried if you've never told them what we've talked about? Because without that, I'm just some guy hanging around you a million miles from home, and who knows what my intentions are. I don't blame them for being worried. I assumed you'd have been open with them about everything we've worked out."

"You blame me?" Frankie asked, biting at the inside of her lip to keep her emotions in check. "You don't understand what it's like to live in a place like Edenville. It's not like the city you grew up in. Everyone always tells me how much potential I have, but there is nothing to do with it there. I need space. I need more than North Carolina. They just don't understand that."

"They don't have to understand it, Frankie, but they deserve to hear it from you. You haven't even canceled your scholarship in North Carolina yet, have you? It's starting to sound like maybe this isn't what you really want."

"Don't say that. I didn't cancel my scholarship because I knew my parents would find out. I wanted to come out here. I wanted you and me to really be together and do something substantial. My parents could see how good we are together, and they'd realize how capable I am. This would help them get used to the idea that I might belong somewhere beyond driving distance from the place I was born. I was trying to be strategic. But I was certainly not changing my mind. You're what I want. This is all I've ever wanted." There was a panic in her voice that made even the waiter look concerned as he silently handed Maxwell the wine list and slipped away.

"Frankie," Maxwell whispered, reaching a hand across the table and covering hers with his, "calm down."

"Isn't this what you want?" she asked, knowing she could not truly brace herself for the answer. "You are about to start law school. You'll have piles of work and all new people in your life. Am I not a part of that equation?"

"You are the whole equation, Frankie," Maxwell insisted. "Since the first time I met you, I knew you were something special. I have a huge journey ahead of me, and every time I close my eyes and think about all I have to do, I think about having you by my side. You understand what it means to be completely focused on something. You know what it's like to put in the hard work for what you want. That's the kind of person I want. I'm only worried that you'll be giving up too much to be there."

"Giving up what?" Frankie asked, raising and then quieting her voice quickly when she remembered they were in a restaurant.

"I already did the college thing, Frankie. I had the fraternity and the parties. I did the dorm and the fun stuff. You're going to miss all that."

"I'm still going to college. You make it sound like you're going to be locking me in a cage somewhere. You know me well enough to know I don't want to be one of those girls running up and down the hallways of a dorm shouting the latest pop song with a gaggle of my classmates. If I wanted keg parties and bonfires I'd have had plenty of opportunities for those back in Edenville. Moving to Arizona and living with you is not giving anything up, it's gaining everything I've wanted for a long time." It was impossible to hide the vulnerability in her voice now. That was the effect Maxwell had on her. He was the one thing that could knock her off her axis, and she both loved and hated it. Being in control was Frankie's drug. She hadn't needed to be a party girl; she got her fix from a good to-do list and a project syllabus. But Maxwell took all that control away. For some unexplainable reason he made her want to be someone she wasn't—a doe-eyed, reckless, runaway girl who'd do anything to be with him.

"We can do this," Maxwell assured her with the smile he always used when Frankie was feeling particularly unsteady. "We'll get through this trip, and then, if you want, I'll go back with you to Edenville. I'll talk to your family about our plans and, even if they're angry, at least we'll be together."

"You would do that?" Frankie watched the waiter take another unsure lap around them, darting away when she leaned in closer to Maxwell across the table. "You'd really subject yourself to their craziness for me?"

"I would," Maxwell answered. "I know this trip won't be exactly what we had planned, but we can still make the best of it. Tomorrow morning I'll pick you up and we can take the two-hour drive to campus and take in all the sights."

"Pick me up from where exactly? We have a hotel room." Frankie felt the ease of his smile wash her away.

"*I* have a hotel room now. Your dad called Shayna's mom and arranged for you to stay at her house. She's expecting you in about an hour."

"Shayna isn't even there. She's gone to her cousin's house for the next three days. That's why we were going to go do all our stuff first and be together before we started working on the story. I'm supposed to go stay at Shayna's house when she isn't even there?" Frankie let the bubbling anger change her face to a hot ember red. They were supposed to go back to the hotel. This was supposed to be their night, a night to remember. The start of something.

"Your dad is expecting you to check in when you get there. If we have any chance of a future that involves your parents' support, this is how it needs to be. It's not like we can't have time for us, we just won't be staying together."

She wanted to scream at the way he was minimizing that momentous fact. Staying together meant far more than he was saying. It was going to be their night to finally take their relationship to the next level. They would share something amazing and then wake up the next morning in each other's arms. How could this not disappoint him? "You're seriously fine with me staying somewhere else? After all the time we've spent waiting?"

"I have no choice but to be fine with it. I'm trying to look at the big picture. I really believe we can have a future together, and I'm not willing to blow that so we can be together right now. Even though, trust me," he squeezed her hand tightly, "I want very much to take you back to the hotel and have the night we imagined. But I'm not willing to trade that for the future I hope we have."

"So what exactly are we going to do? Can we hold hands? Are we dating? What the hell are we allowed to do?" Frankie felt the grip on her daydreams slipping away. She'd been imagining this trip for so long, and it was dissolving in front of her eyes.

"Your dad didn't exactly give me a list of do's and don'ts. We need to treat this as delicately as possible. I don't want your dad to have to worry for a minute about what we're doing out here. You stay at Shayna's, and we'll spend a lot of time together." She had to give Maxwell credit for his optimism. Another guy would certainly have been pissed at how all of this had gone down. But that was what she liked about him. He saw more than the moment they were living in; he could consider how it would impact the future. "Now I think we should stop talking and order before our waiter wears a hole in the carpet doing laps around us."

She let out a tiny laugh and tried to smile through the pain she was feeling in her heart. It took all her strength to keep her eyes from falling toward the table and to keep her lips from pouting like a child. If she did those things it would only make her look immature. She had to smile at with this new plan as though she'd helped to craft it herself. She'd have to ignore the feeling that her heart had been butchered. Her dreams felt like they'd been dismantled, pulled apart by the greedy hands of everyone who thought they knew better than she did. But none of that would matter. It was all about keeping her head up and pretending she could roll with the punches when she'd much rather be throwing punches right now.

"So we're good?" Maxwell asked, flashing his hazel eyes at her as though everything was going to be fine.

"So good," she lied, lifting her menu to cover her face. "So, so good."

Chapter Four

"All right, we can fix this," Jules said as she paced around her mother's kitchen. "We can hire a private investigator out there to keep an eye on her. Oh hell, I'll just go out there myself." She grabbed her car keys as though there would be a plane waiting for her the moment she got to the airport.

"Relax," Bobby said, snatching the keys and turning her shoulders away from the door, toward a kitchen chair.

"How long have you been married to Piper, Bobby? Have you seriously not learned how dangerous it is to tell a frantic woman to relax?" Jules had her fists clenched as though she might sock him right in the nose.

Betty brought her a big glass of sweet tea poured over a pile of ice. "Drink this and take a deep breath," she instructed. "You know as well as the rest of us that if you go out there right now you'll be the bad guy, and you'll be paying for it for years to come."

"Then I'll go and not tell her I'm there. If I stay close by in case she needs me, then that won't be so bad."

"You have a life here, Jules," Michael said, dismissing her idea. "We're not going to drop everything to go chase her."

"I'm hearing a lot of objections but no suggestions," Jules said, scanning everyone in the room with a scrutinizing glare.

"Unfortunately there is only one thing to do." Betty sighed. "We wait. Pray that everything you've filled her with over the years is enough to sustain her while you can't be with her. Everyone goes through this."

"I never put you through this," Jules shot back, knowing she'd never run away like this when she was young.

"How quickly you forget," Betty cackled. "I vividly remember you going off and marrying that fool Scott just to spite me."

"I was in my twenties by then," Jules defended, but she could already tell by the glint in her mother's eye that she would not win.

"That only tells me you were dumber longer," Betty countered. "But it doesn't make what you're going through right now any easier. So I'll tell you what you can do. You can depend on the people in this room to help you through it. We'll listen when you're scared. Pour you a shot when your nerves are raging. That's about the best you can do for the next . . . I don't know, five years or so. You've got to treat it like you do your nose."

Every eye in the room turned toward her, and their faces made it unnecessary to ask the obvious question.

"Oh come on, you know. Your eyes see your nose all the time. It's right in the way of everything you try to look at but your brain finds a way to ignore it. Don't you people know science? All I'm saying is the worry is going to be there all the time but you've got to find a way to look beyond it."

"Do you have a book of these things written down somewhere Betty?" Piper asked, crossing her eyes for a second to get a good look at her own nose.

"There isn't a book big enough for all my wisdom," Betty teased as she wrapped her arms around her daughter and squeezed tightly. "I'm sorry you're going through this. It's not fair to you."

"I want to strangle her," Jules admitted. "Then I want to hug her and never let her go. Then I want to punish her forever and tell her how much I love her. I'm a mess."

Betty kissed the crown of her daughter's head and whispered into her hair, "No honey, you're not a mess. You're a mother."

Chapter Five

Shayna's mother, Lila, was sweet, but her tight hug nearly suffocated Frankie. Like a cobra she coiled herself around her newly arrived guest and gave no sign of letting go. "Frankie, we are so excited to have you. Shayna mentioned you were coming for a visit to do some research, but I'm thrilled to have you here so early."

"Well, I'm sure my father filled you in," Frankie groaned, as she wiggled her way out of the tight hug.

"I'm sorry things didn't work out the way you planned," Lila sympathized as she maternally stroked Frankie's hair. "Your father just wants what's best for you. I promise to make your stay here as fun as possible. And Maxwell is welcome here whenever I'm home."

"That's really nice, Mrs. Kosaian," Frankie said, trying to make sure the grinding of her teeth wasn't loud enough to be heard.

"Oh stop, please call me Lila. Having you here is the very least I can do. Your father has done more for Shayna than her own father ever has. I always knew she was in good hands when she would be staying with you on your school travels. It's very scary to have a wildly intelligent daughter when you live in such an oppressed area like this. I always worried she'd never get the opportunity to reach her potential, but with your family's help she has. I'll be forever indebted for that." Lila's face was weathered for a woman only in her forties. She looked like she'd lived her whole life outdoors. Her leathery brown skin was creased with wrinkles. The bags beneath her eyes looked like lumps of stress that had piled up and refused to leave. She was tiny, and her ragged clothes hung loosely. But her genuine kindness forced Frankie to relax.

"I love Shayna, my whole family does. She's been my best friend and travel buddy for the last four years, and I can tell you those trips would have been painfully dull without her. She's going to have a really bright future, and that has much more to do with you than anyone else. She admires you so much." Frankie dropped her bag from her shoulder as Lila moved in for another grateful hug.

"You are such a magnificent girl. You are welcome here, and we're going to make sure you have everything you need. Tao, come on out here." When Lila finally released Frankie she called out again over her shoulder, "Tao, please do not make me come in your filthy room and drag you out here."

"I'm right here," a gravelly voice bellowed back as he stepped into the living room. Frankie knew Tao to be Shayna's younger brother, but she'd never met him. She'd only heard the horror stories of the trouble he caused. He was nothing at all like she'd expected. Shayna had always described him as a pest and a pain in her ass, and while Frankie knew he was only a year younger than she and Shayna, she had visions of her little brother, Ian, an eleven-year-old who couldn't keep his sticky hands off her diary. He certainly was nothing at all like this man who just stepped in the room and seemed to take up half of it with his wide shoulders. Tao's hair was shaggy, dark, and thick. But she didn't look at it very long, instead her eyes were drawn to his bare chest. He had no shirt on, and Frankie quickly averted her eyes. But it was too late, she'd already caught a glimpse of his well-defined muscles and cocoa skin.

Switching to a different language, Lila's voice raised a few octaves, and though Frankie couldn't decipher anything she was saying, it was easy to infer it had something to do with putting on a damn shirt. Frankie couldn't agree more.

Tao scurried back to his room, waving his hands like he was batting away her angry words. "Excuse me, I didn't realize our rich little white princess had arrived," Tao shot back in English and then dodged his mother's swiping slap as they stumbled back into the cramped and gloomy living room.

A final rant in her other language and Lila seemed to settle as Tao reluctantly apologized. "I'm so sorry," Lila apologized further, "Tao can be a bit brash sometimes. But he won't give you any more trouble. He'll be the most accommodating host you can imagine. Isn't that right?" She glared at her son and waited for his nod of agreement. When he finally gave it she turned her voice back to her normal singsong and grabbed her coat. "I work third shift at the truck stop coffee house. I hate to leave you, but Tao here will get you whatever you need. I'll be back in the morning, but then I usually sleep for a while. You're welcome to my car for your research if you need it."

"Maxwell will be back in the morning. We're working the story together. I shouldn't need the car at all, but I appreciate it."

Looking down at her watch Lila sprang quickly into action, obviously running late. Glaring one more time at her son, she turned and headed out the door.

"I need the car tomorrow," Tao announced as he pulled his shirt off again and flopped onto the couch.

"Are you going clothes shopping? You seem to be having a hard time finding a shirt you want to keep on," Frankie nipped as she pulled her phone from her bag. Dialing her father's number, she pressed the phone to her ear and drew in a deep breath. Before her father could say anything she cut in. "I'm at Shayna's. Maxwell is at the hotel off the reservation, and you win."

"I wasn't trying to win, Frankie," Michael replied solemnly. "I'm trying to protect you."

"From Maxwell? Do you honestly think I need to be protected from Maxwell? He's a great guy who you have actually said on multiple occasions that you really like. He's going to be in law school soon, and he has his life figured out. I don't need protection from him." There was still so much fight left in Frankie she knew before even dialing the phone there would be an argument.

"I know that. Maxwell is an upstanding guy, which is why he did what I asked tonight. He knows it's the right thing for you to stay at your friend's house and not with him in some hotel. I'm not protecting you from him; I'm protecting you from your own mistakes."

"My own mistakes?" Frankie demanded, tossing a hand up in the air angrily. "That's great. Do you just intend to follow me around for the rest of my life and make sure I never take a risk, never fall? I'm not a toddler, Dad. You can let go of my hands. I've got this walking thing down now."

"Get some rest," Michael sighed. "Check in tomorrow. Make sure you're being polite to Lila as well. She doesn't deserve any attitude."

"Eight hours enough sleep, Dad, or should I shoot for nine? I know how to be a gracious houseguest, and Lila hasn't done anything to screw up my life, so she'll be safe."

"I love you, sweetheart. I'm sorry you can't see how much right now, but we all love you."

Ending the call, she slammed her phone down on the end table next to her and sent a lamp flying to the ground with a thud. A thud was better than a shatter, but she still felt terrible as she tried to stand it back up quickly. "I'm sorry," she repeated frantically. "I don't think it's broken."

"It's a piece of crap anyway," Tao offered with a shrug of his bare shoulders. "Everything in here is."

"It's a nice house," Frankie said, pushing her bangs away from her eyes and wishing this day would just end. She'd spent hours on a train and then time arguing with everyone she loved. She had, of course, anticipated all the fighting, but she assumed it would end with her lying in Maxwell's arms in the hotel room. To have the arguing without the reward was like a diet without the weight loss. Pointless.

"It's a shithole like every other house on this reservation." Tao tucked his arms behind his head and continued to stare at Frankie as she tried to put the lamp back exactly where it had been. "So not getting along with the rest of the Richie Rich family? That must be why I've been ordered to babysit you."

"Babysit me?" Frankie's rage began to build again. If she didn't get it under control she might hurl this stupid lamp right at his head.

"Yep," Tao grinned. "I'm supposed to make sure you stay in my sight tonight and don't run off to be with your boyfriend or something. But I'm not supposed to tell you that."

"Keep up the good work," Frankie grumbled as she slung her bag over her shoulder again. "Just point me to Shayna's room."

"You're standing in it," Tao chuckled. "Well, actually you have to pull this couch out to make the lumpy bed, then you'd be standing in it."

"Shayna doesn't have her own room?" Frankie asked, hoping that Tao was just screwing with her and sad if he wasn't.

"I'm sure when she was traveling the country with you on the debate team and all that crap, she made you think she was just like you, but she isn't. She sleeps on a lumpy pullout couch in the living room. Still want to be friends with her?"

"She could sleep on a pallet in the alley and I'd still be friends with Shayna. She's kind and compassionate. Apparently it doesn't run in the family."

"Ouch," Tao shot back mockingly, grabbing his heart like he'd been struck by an arrow.

"But why does she sleep out here?" Frankie asked, assessing how big the rest of the house was by what she'd seen on the outside.

"Because we're poor. Because everyone here is poor. What kind of stupid question is that?" Tao shot back. He had a constant brooding scowl that was made more intense by the depth of his dark eyes. His high cheekbones and rigid chin were just like Shayna's and a clear indication of his heritage, but the anger in his brow was all his own. His sister was bubbly, her optimistic smile her favorite accessory to wear.

"I meant why does she sleep out here while you have your own room? You should sleep out here." Frankie perched her hand on her hip and stuck her chin out challengingly.

With that Tao's face went to stone in a way that made Frankie shiver. She'd just struck a chord that clearly didn't sit well with her already annoyed host. Instead of marking that off as a victory, she felt a pang of guilt and tried to change the subject.

"I just want to go read somewhere. Is there anywhere I can be alone?" Frankie asked, pulling a book from her bag with a huff.

"What's the deal exactly?" Tao asked. "You show up here all pissed off, my mom makes me keep an eye on you, and you're fighting with your parents. I bet that's a juicy story."

"I'm not here to entertain you with the screwed-up details of my derailed plans. Apparently I'm here to be watched closely by you so I don't accidently live my life. But why would I bother doing that anyway? My father is already doing that for me." Frankie flopped on the couch with a huff and prayed it was slightly more comfortable when pulled out to a bed than it was in its current rock-solid position.

"You came out here to be with your boyfriend, and Daddy doesn't like him? Is he a drunk or a convict or something?" Tao leaned forward as though he couldn't wait to devour the salacious details. He looked like a hungry dog with a steak dangling in front of him.

With a sudden pang of anger she felt the need to defend Maxwell. "He's neither of those things. He's well-read, incredibly educated, and on a great career path. My father just can't stop picturing me in pigtails, coloring on my grandmother's front porch, long enough to realize I'm an adult."

"How exactly is an eighteen-year-old already on a great career path?" Tao asked his brows furrowing skeptically. "Is this kid one of those who graduate college at fifteen or something, a super genius? Because those kids are always weird."

"He's not eighteen; he's twenty-one and about to start law school in the fall. He just transferred to a university here in Arizona. I'm going to go to school here for journalism too. We're going to live together. This trip was supposed to be about us starting to work out all the details. Instead, I'm stuck here like a prisoner."

"Oh I get it now, he's too old for you," Tao said with a look as though it all made sense now.

"You don't even know him," Frankie shot back loudly.

"I don't need to know him because I know this crazy little thing called math. I'm with your dad on this one. Richie Rich knows what he's doing."

"Let's get one thing straight right now. My family is *not* pretentious. The money we have belonged to my father's parents, and we don't ever use it on ourselves. We never have. It goes to scholarships my family funds and donations to causes we believe in. Our house isn't all that much bigger than yours. We live a very modest life; my parents have earned everything they have, and so have I. I worked just as hard in my grandmother's restaurant as I did at school. Not to mention all my volunteer hours. You must know all about that, it's kind of like court-mandated community service except I did it by choice. You can't even imagine what I had to accomplish for my scholarship, and I'm not taking a dime from my family for college. So drop the nicknames and judgments, considering you know nothing about me." There was a rattle in her voice that she hated. It undermined her point and made her sound like she was about to cry, likely because she felt like she was.

"Sorry," Tao choked out. "You've always done so much for my sister I figured you must be, like, really rich or something. All the really rich people I've ever seen are all the same. Shayna always said you were really nice, but I figured you were just treating her like some charity case."

"I met Shayna when we were in Washington for a spelling bee. Some girls were teasing me because of my red hair and my braces, and Shayna stuck up for me. I felt so terrible about myself, and she cheered me up. When my dad met her he saw how bright and kind she was, and he wanted to help her have opportunities to succeed."

"He sounds like a good guy. The kind of guy who would worry about you, I guess." Tao leaned back in his chair looking far less arrogant now.

"Whatever, I don't want to talk about it anymore. I just want to . . ." Frankie let her voice trail off as she buried her face in her hands, wishing she could fix everything. She wished she could be with Maxwell right now. That would be the magic wand to fix all this nonsense.

"So you're not really here for research or whatever?" Tao asked, squirming in his seat, clearly uncomfortable with the thought of an upset girl on his couch.

"What?" Frankie asked, rubbing at the painful thumping in her temples. "Oh yeah, I mean I came out here for a story. Shayna always talked about the reservation and the challenges here. There's been lots of times over the years she's used it as an example to make a debate point or cite a precedent. She told me about something a while back, and it stuck with me. I think there is more to the story, and Maxwell and I are going to hunt it down and document it all. I've got this whistleblower website that's interested in the content I was going to pitch. The contact I have there was confident it could go viral."

"Why?" Tao asked, looking like she'd just told him she wanted to polka dance on the moon.

"Because I want to be a journalist, and I'd like to make a name for myself in the state I'll be going to school in. Maxwell and I, we have plans to do big things together, and it starts here. Right on this reservation." Frankie drew in a deep breath and hopped to her feet. She moved across the room toward the cracked front window and stared out into the night.

"What exactly do you know about this reservation? What do you know about the Tewapia people or our culture?" Tao stood, and she could feel him inching closer. His shadow cast over her like a blanket of darkness.

"I've read a lot about the Native American population and history. Not specific to this area but in general." Frankie turned toward Tao and stared up at his stoic expression. He had the look of someone from a different time. There was an ancient air about his features that made her think of something she'd seen in one of her history books. She focused on his face, considering she was only inches away from his bare chest.

"You plan to spend time on this reservation, asking questions and investigating things?" Tao questioned, a new lift in his shoulders said he meant business. This question was a challenge.

"Part of our time will be on the reservation. It's a cold case that took place off reservation, so I'm guessing we'll split our time," she answered slowly as if he might interrupt and shout at her at any moment.

"No one here will talk to you. You know nothing about anything that's important to them, and they'll take one look at you and see that. It's pointless." Tao folded his arms across his chest and raised a challenging eyebrow at her.

"I told you I've read extensively." Frankie cocked an eyebrow in the way she always did when about to engage in a debate.

"Come out with me tonight," Tao challenged, raising one of his thick midnight black brows back at her.

"No," she answered instantly, practically before the words had left his mouth. "I've had a long trip and a miserable day. I'm not going to go party with your buddies over a keg in the woods. Thanks anyway." That thank you was not meant to have a sliver of gratitude.

"Who said that's where I'm going? You would rather sit in this dilapidated house all night reading and feeling sorry for yourself? You need to lighten up."

That was it. The phrase she'd heard over and over again for the last five years. Maybe it was the exhaustion, the backache, or the disappointment, but that was the last straw. Perhaps she was being fueled by the smug look on this jerk's face, but hearing the same thing for the hundredth time, made something snap.

"I am not some uptight prude who sits around reading because she's completely unaware of what it's like to live it up with a bunch of morons. Every choice I make, every hour of work I've put in, is a conscious decision because I am determined to have options for my future. Do you honestly think you are the first guy to assume he's going to give me some kind of awakening? This isn't an angsty teen movie where you get me to pull the ponytail from my hair and take off my reading glasses, changing me into a beautiful fun-loving swan. I'm not going to run off into the woods with you and go skinny dipping in the pond or sit around a bonfire drinking. My life isn't lacking anything, and I'm not waiting for someone to fix me. I'm not broken. I'm determined. I'm driven. And believe it or not, I'm happy with that. So I won't lighten up." She drew in a quick breath, realizing too late she hadn't done so since she started her speech.

"Easy," Tao replied, raising his hands up disarmingly. "I think you've misjudged me."

"If I did, you started it," Frankie nipped back, knowing how painfully immature her response was. Before Tao could pounce on her idiotic reply, her phone began to ring. It was Maxwell. Thank heavens for that. What she needed was a pep talk from the guy who knew her best.

Chapter Six

"You shouldn't sit out here on your own at night. The desert is full of all sorts of wildlife you don't know anything about," Tao warned as he stepped out the squeaking front door of his house and stood behind Frankie, who was perched on the bottom step in the dark.

"Fine," she choked out, and she immediately wanted to kick herself for the fluster in her voice that clearly indicated she was crying.

"What's the matter?" Tao asked nervously as he lowered himself to the step behind her.

"You wouldn't understand. I don't feel like arguing anymore so I would rather just not talk about it." Frankie used her sleeve to clean her face even though the rough edge of her shirt made her eyes sting more.

"Even if I don't get why you're crying, I promise I won't be a dick. You don't grow up in a house with two women and find it easy to walk away when someone's crying. I'm not going to be able to leave you alone, so you might as well talk about it."

"Everything is a mess," Frankie sobbed, louder than she meant to. "That was Maxwell on the phone, and he got a call from the law firm he was trying to intern with this summer. Originally he'd been put on a waiting list, but they called him tonight and told me they have a spot for him if he can start tomorrow. Otherwise they'll go to the next person on the list."

"That sucks," Tao replied, sounding pretty confident in his answer until he saw Frankie spin around abruptly.

"No, it's great. This firm will help him network and build a career. It's an opportunity that could change his entire life. He's so lucky to have gotten that call."

"Oh," Tao tried again, nodding his head as though he understood. "So that's good news. You are crying tears of joy?"

"No," Frankie groaned. "It's great news for him, but it means I'll barely see him during this trip. We were supposed to work this story together. We were going to be this great team. We were going to stay at a hotel near here and visit the university. There was even time set aside for us to look at apartments and furniture. My dad intimidated Maxwell out of doing any of that on this trip, and now the little bit we had left to hang onto is gone."

"How much time could it take up really?" Tao asked, shrugging as though none of this was as big a deal as she was making it. "Can't you still do some stuff on the weekends or at night? The university is only a couple hours away."

"This law firm will practically own him. He'll be getting calls day and night, and he won't want to be more than a few minutes from the place, even on the weekends. I could ask him and maybe he would, but the whole time he'd be distracted. I had everything planned for this trip. It was supposed to mean so much, and now it means nothing." Frankie buried her face back in her hands and let the tears flow. She wasn't one to break down in front of a stranger, but the tidal wave of emotions had swept her away.

"What's the story you came out here to research? Doesn't that still exist even without your boyfriend?" Tao moved down one step, close enough for his knee to be near her heavy and tired head. She could hear the little

47

prickly edge in his voice when he said the word *boyfriend*, but she could appreciate he was trying.

"It does," Frankie admitted. "It's still important to me. It still matters." She sniffled and wiped her face again as she sat up and turned to look at Tao. "I just really wanted to do this with Maxwell."

"I might be a little out of my depth here. I feel like there's probably something really sensitive to say right now, but it's not coming to me. The only thing I can think to say is, *that sucks*, which didn't work last time." Tao punctuated his offering with a tiny smile, and she couldn't help but smile back a little. Maybe it was because she'd already spent nearly an hour with him, and this was the first time he didn't look annoyed.

"Actually, that might be the only suitable response for this situation. I'm just disappointed." She wiped again at her eyes as she tried to get her emotions in check. "I'm never like this by the way. I don't cry over every little thing."

"So your story involves the reservation?" Tao pushed on, grinding the figurative clutch as he tried to quickly change gears on this conversation. Frankie gracefully allowed him to.

"Yes. It's mainly about a journalistic bias surrounding media that covers the reservations. You don't have your own media outlets here so you depend on the ones off the reservation. I was going to cover how you aren't accurately represented by their stories, and in many cases it's downright misinformation that's printed. There's this cold case going back almost two decades that highlights the disparities and tensions between the reservation and the surrounding towns through media coverage." Her voice grew stronger as she tried to root herself back into the one thing she could still control.

"Then you need to understand the Tewapia culture. You need to know how to speak to people here without offending them. I can help with that. I know you already said no, but I'm going to ask you again. Come out with me tonight. I'll help you. It's really all I was offering the first time." Tao used his knee to nudge her shoulder lightly. "Before, I wasn't trying to say you didn't know how to have fun, and I certainly wasn't trying to skinny dip with you. We don't even have ponds around here."

Frankie laughed before she remembered to be sad, and that felt nice. "On one condition."

"What's that?" Tao asked, looking like he may rescind his offer if he didn't like what she had to say. He had an air about him that, if challenged, he would walk away. His expression said he wouldn't be held hostage by someone's terms, but luckily she wasn't asking for too much.

"You have to wear a shirt." Frankie let her smile grow full now and watched him roll his eyes as he hopped to his feet.

"Just put some sneakers on, we're going out into the desert." He was gone, disappearing back into the house before she could ask if he was serious. Curiosity propelled her forward as she followed him and dug her sneakers out of her bag.

"Is it safe?" she asked, studying his face to get a read on his trustworthiness.

"If you're with me you'll be fine. I've spent my entire life in this desert. There have been plenty of times I headed out for days at a time to clear my head and get back to nature. I know each creature like it's my brother."

Tao slipped a shirt over his head and wrestled his big feet into his ripped sneakers. Frankie noted this was the first thing he'd said all night that sounded authentic to who he was. Everything else she originally read as arrogance, in retrospect, now seemed more like bravado. But this talk of the creatures in the desert and his connection to them seemed unguarded and genuine.

Frankie pulled on her pink hooded sweatshirt and wished it was one of Maxwell's college ones instead. This one smelled only like her own jasmine perfume and wasn't roomy like his. But that was a metaphor for this entire trip. She'd have to find a way to feel good in her own skin, just her without him and his things. Zipping it, determined to focus on her other goals, she took a step out into the night, following closely behind Tao.

She watched his feet move like nothing she'd ever seen before. Swift and light, he seemed to float across the dirt, not disturbing anything. The beam of his flashlight danced in front of him, catching the shadow of a cactus and then a prickly bush. The farther they walked, the darker it seemed to become. The tiny rundown houses, just like the one they had left, fell away and all that remained was nature. Noise seemed to evaporate into the blanket of stars that burned brighter than Frankie had ever seen before. She knew logically these were the same stars she'd spent her life looking at, but tonight she felt as though she were seeing them for the first time.

They approached a cluster of rocks the size of a two-story house, and Tao intentionally walked toward them. "Can you climb?" he asked, pointing the flashlight toward her.

"Can I climb what? These rocks? I don't know. I used to climb trees, but I haven't in a long time. Is it like that?" She stared at the rocks with a look of unease.

"It's not at all like climbing a tree, but you can do it," he assured her as he pointed the light at the rock and gestured for her to give it a try.

"I appreciate your confidence in me, but it's misplaced. If I fall I could break my neck. It's just a bunch of rocks, why do we need to climb it? Can't we go around?"

"Shh." He silenced her with a wave of his hand and she froze, totally uneasy about her surroundings. "Did you hear that rattle? Sounds like a good sized snake." He pointed toward a rock and encouraged her again. She hadn't heard the rattle the first time so she hesitated, unsure if he was joking or just trying to get her to do what he wanted. But the second the noise came again she took hold of the rock and began climbing as though her life depended on it.

"See you just needed the right reason to climb. Don't worry, I'm right behind you." She felt his arms on either side of her, ready to catch her if she slipped. He scaled the rock as though it were an extension of his body. When she froze and had to think where to grab next, his arm reached up and pointed to the perfect spot, his bicep flashing under the moonlight.

It felt like one of her legs might slide off, and she'd be left dangling off the side of the large rock formation. But she didn't slip.

Tao had the flashlight hanging from a string between his teeth now, and the bouncing of the light was just enough to help guide her. She propelled herself up the side of the rock until she was shimmying her way over the top, sliding on her belly, and then hopping to her feet victoriously. She'd done nothing so far in Arizona until this moment. Finally she'd accomplished something.

"That was amazing!" she shouted, her voice echoing through the expanse of the desert night. Covering her mouth she hunched her shoulders apologetically.

"No one to apologize to out here," he assured her as they took a moment to look out over the moonlit expanse in front of them.

"I didn't expect you to climb that well," Tao admitted. "But I'm glad you did. It's twice as hard to get up here with a girl on my back."

"Bring a lot of girls up here?" Frankie teased with her leading question, but he didn't bite. He just shrugged and grabbed her hand. The touch was enough of a surprise that she considered pulling away, but her fingers were cold, this rock was high, and his hand was warm and safe. All were rational reasons to keep holding on. He led her to a pile of wood meticulously arranged for a fire. He let her hand go and gestured for her to sit as he pulled matches from his pocket.

"My ancestors would prefer I sit out here rubbing two sticks together, but who has that kind of time?" As he struck the match his face lit orange for a moment. He watched the flame, then quickly tossed the match down. The wood crackled slightly, smoked, and the fire took hold.

Here they were on top of a giant rock formation she'd just climbed, sitting around a fire in what she could only describe as the quietest place on earth. Frankie felt peace fall upon her. "Thanks for this," she said quietly as she stared at him across the fire. She doubted he even knew what her gratitude was for, but he nodded his reply anyway.

"What do you think of this reservation?" Tao asked, his black eyes dancing with the light of the fire as he stared intensely at her.

"I honestly didn't see much of it on the way in. I was distracted. But from what I did see, this is a very peaceful, quiet place. Not that much different from where I live." She assumed he wanted her to acknowledge how this place was on the poverty line, teetering on the edge of despair. That hadn't been lost on her; she just didn't want to paint it with such a broad brush considering she hadn't seen that much of it.

"Close your eyes," he insisted, and she obeyed, understanding he was trying to explain something to her and would only do so on his terms. "Where is the place you feel safest in the world? When you consider being happy and loved what images come to mind? Where is your heart's home? Tell me." His voice barely sounded like the one she'd heard over the last two hours. His arrow-straight back and serious tone were different versions of himself she hadn't expected.

A picture of Maxwell flashed before her mind's eye but quickly evaporated. Though he made her feel happy, she couldn't actually say he was the one place she felt at home. Instead she saw the place she'd learned to tie her shoes and make biscuits. Clear as day, as though she were standing there now, she could see it. "My grandmother's house. We all go there, my whole family, all the time. I practically grew up there."

"Tell me what you see so I can see it too," Tao instructed, but Frankie felt her cheeks flush. This was all so different than she expected. She had misjudged Tao, assuming he had the emotional depth of a shallow puddle, but here they were on top of a giant rock, eyes closed, having a moment.

"Her name is Betty, and she's the best person I've ever known. Her house is set back from the street. There's a long dirt driveway and a stone wall that runs the length of it. The birds sound like a choir most days and the grass is high. It has weeds but pretty ones that dot yellow and purple all the way through. I see everyone is gathered out on the porch, and they're laughing at something my brother Ian just did. Then all the kids—my little cousins and brother—take off into the yard and start playing tag." Frankie felt a warmth in her chest that she tried to blame on the now roaring fire she was perched next to. But she knew better. It was hard to think of everyone back home and how she'd hurt each of them. Regret was a hungry beast and it kept trying to eat away at her confidence.

"Out in the distance, at the end of that long driveway there is now a crowd of people, strangers," Tao said coolly, his voice sending a chill up her spine as though he were telling a spooky story at camp. "Their sheer numbers are enough to be intimidating, but it's more the look on their faces that unsettles you."

"Yes," Frankie whispered, seeing what Tao was explaining as if it were plain as day.

"Someone goes out to see what's happening," Tao continues.

"My Uncle Bobby would," Frankie suggests. "He's a police officer. He'd want to be the first one out there."

"The crowd ignores him and moves in closer, pushing him back toward you. They tell you all they want your front yard. They want to live there now. At first you are all enraged, but soon you see the weapons these people have and realize you have no choice. You give them your front yard. Soon they have built structures that block the sun from your house. They bring sicknesses you and your family have never had to deal with before. And when they become hungry, they encroach even more. Now they are in your grandmother's house. They are in your fridge. In your room. Maybe some of your family fights back and are injured or killed. They want your house. They are taking your house. There is nothing you can do."

"No," Frankie whispered back. "They had the whole yard."

"That is not enough," Tao says angrily, sending her jumping. "You and your family are moved to a closet with only the belongings you can carry. Shoved inside this small space you are told you cannot leave. But the children, they will be spared. They'll be taken with this crowd to a new school. They'll be taught the ways of these strangers, and they will be punished if they speak of the days of playing tag or telling jokes. They must change to survive, so they do. And in this closet people become sad. They become disconnected from everything they used to do out on the porch and in the front yard. They suffer. They die. All the while the house is being destroyed and changed. It's made bigger; it's made dirty and overcrowded. Everything beautiful about it is gone. The children return changed, ignoring the joy that came before the strangers arrived. Forgetting all that used to be a part of their lives so they cannot share it with their own children, completely erasing the happiness and peace that once was. And you are in this closet."

"That's horrible," Frankie moaned sadly.

"Your grandmother's home is gone. Your family is dismantled and fractured. Your way of life and freedom are snatched away. You are in a closet." Tao's words are almost a song now as he chants this nightmare out loud. "You must be like this crowd of strangers, or you must stay in your closet."

"There have to be other choices," Frankie begged, squeezing her eyes closed even tighter.

"Or you can die," Tao explained somberly.

"I can't imagine," Frankie breathed out on the verge of tears.

"Do you love the closet?" Tao asked, reaching across and touching her arm gently as she opened her eyes. "Do you love the closet?" he asked again.

"No," she replied angrily. "Why would I love the closet? It's a prison. I loved my grandmother's house and my family the way it was before. I hate the closet. It's a piece of my grandmother's house, but it's not the same."

"That's why I don't love the reservation. That's why many people here do not. It's why they drink and smoke and hide. It's why they fail and hate. But it's also why some try to carry on the old ways. It's why they sing the songs and do the powwows. They tell the old stories so that even in the closet, history is not lost. I am Tewapia. For thousands of years that meant something. Now I don't know what it means anymore. I can live in the closet where there is nothing, I can be like my sister and live in their world, or I can die. Right now that's what it means to be Tewapia."

"I'm sorry," Frankie offered, suddenly flooded with guilt for not only her ignorance but for her association, even if just by skin color, to the people responsible.

"The way you feel right now, hold onto that. That is what people will see in your eyes, on your face when you try to talk to them. That is the understanding you must have in order to be accepted here."

Frankie imagined bottling this knowledge and tapping into it when needed. Tao had given her the gift of perspective, and she would use that.

"There is more," he said, interrupting her thought. "A Tewapia person will tell you what you are meant to know. That means you do not ask follow-up questions. If he tells you the stream flows east, you do not ask how quickly."

"But," Frankie started and stopped short when she saw the stern look on Tao's face. "You have to understand," she tried again. "That goes against every one of my journalistic instincts. I have always asked questions, hundreds of them, until people are tired of me. It's kind of my thing. What if I need to know how fast the river moves?"

"You don't or else he'd have told you when you asked about the river. It's a matter of trust. The elders here know more than you, so you have to believe they know how much information you need."

Frankie drew in a deep breath. This was a tall order for an inquisitive girl who was trying to dig up information and opinions.

"Also," Tao added, "body language is its own language here. You may feel like someone is ignoring you by not speaking, but you are not listening properly. Try to watch more than hear. Read people more than see them. Do not shake hands—it is thought to be aggressive. Do not touch anything that looks as though it may be sacred . . . actually don't touch anything. Everything is sacred. If you are offered something, take it, even if you don't want it. That includes anything from a glass of water to a recently killed rattlesnake, which is a sign of friendship. Everything means something. No photographs. No taking notes while someone is talking. If you are listening properly, you'll remember everything."

"I was not prepared for all of this," Frankie stumbled out. "There are a lot of things I can do to screw this up."

"There are," Tao agreed. "But if they see respect in your eyes, they will forgive many things. This place is not a tourist attraction. We are not zoo animals. Our traditions are not things to gawk at on your school vacation. It's not all feathers in the hair and tapping our hands to our mouths as we dance around a fire. We were here thousands of years before you. We were tortured, assimilated, and exterminated, and we are clutching on to the last remnants of our history. If that is the way you look at us, they will see that."

Frankie nodded her head as though she understood, but really she was overwhelmed. It wasn't just the litany of offenses she might accidently commit; it was the person sitting before her, trying to teach. Shayna had always talked about where she was from in general terms. Looking at Tao, Frankie could not only see his passion for his people, she could feel it buzzing around them. This kid who seemed like he didn't give a shit about anything suddenly seemed to care deeply about something she knew little about.

She was disappointed about what had happened today with Maxwell and pissed at her family, but maybe with Tao's help, all was still salvageable.

Chapter Seven

Frankie hadn't really sat silently before, but after the fourth time Tao shushed her, she got the hint. She stared at the stars then at the fire, and occasionally she glanced quickly at his face.

"What are you thinking," he finally asked when he caught her appraising him.

"Nothing," she shot back defensively.

"I highly doubt that. You don't strike me as the kind of person who can think about nothing. It takes years of practice and meditation, I can assure you. You must be thinking about this story of yours."

Anxious to get his scrutinizing eyes off her after being caught staring, she agreed. "Yes. It's very interesting. Seventeen years ago a Tewapia woman was killed."

Tao narrowed his chocolate eyes to slits, and she froze. "Of course. Danyia. That's a very controversial topic here."

"I would think so, considering how it was handled and covered in the media. The man who killed her was her boyfriend, Denver Stills, and he reportedly died in a car accident on the day a warrant was issued for his arrest. There was more coverage of his car accident than there was of a Danyia's murder."

"Danyia's murder is something that troubles many people to this day. I was born that year so I've only heard the stories, but they are plentiful. I'm friendly with her mother. People say she was pretty normal before the murder; now she's a bit cracked."

"Shayna didn't mention that you knew the family of the Danyia."

"Typical," Tao grunted as he poked the fire with a stick and sent the embers dancing in the dark toward the expansive desert sky.

"Why do you seem so mad at Shayna? I've known her for years; she's really sweet and very smart."

"I never said my sister was unkind, more like ungrateful. She takes every opportunity to leave this place and has never taken the time to learn much about her own culture and ancestors. She acts as though she's too good for her own home." Tao's brows knit together in a scowl, and Frankie fought the urge to race to her friend's defense.

"She's always very proud of her heritage when she talks about it to others. I've seen her speak eloquently in many debates about it. She's proud. You shouldn't be too hard on her."

"Most of this started when she first met you. After that she wanted to spend more and more time off the reservation, and she took every chance she got to be with you and your family," Tao explained.

"That's why you were so pissed at me when I got here? You blame me for ruining your sister? I can assure you I don't have that much power. If I did I'd be wielding it in cooler ways."

Tao loosened the figurative screws on his jaw. "It's not like I don't want her to do well. I think it's great she's going to college in the fall. One of us should have the chance."

"Why can't both of you?" Frankie asked, not willing to accept he couldn't attend college if he really wanted to.

"You have another year right? You're a senior in the fall?"

"No, I don't think I'm going back to school in the fall." Tao stood and grabbed another log from the pile to his left, trying to look busier than he really was.

"You're not going to finish high school?" Frankie scoffed. "You have to be kidding. Trying to get a job without a degree is statistically more difficult."

Tao grunted an annoyed laugh and shot his dark eyes her way. "That voice in your head, it's never told you something is impossible has it? The people in your life, I bet they never once used the word *can't* around you. I get why you're so optimistic and determined, but don't get the idea that it comes from your fierce character or something. You're so tough and capable because of your environment and support. It's easy to succeed when you have all the advantages you do. Take that out and you might not be so invincible."

"I've done plenty on my own. I've never relied on my parents for my grades or motivation to stay focused on what's important to me. I did those things." Frankie felt like she was on a roller coaster, slowly climbing hills of admiration for Tao and then shooting down hills of disdain.

"All I'm saying is when you don't have to worry about your next meal, or if the roof in your house will stay up another year, it's easier to succeed. When everything else is taken care of, staying focused is your only job. I have other jobs, other responsibilities. I'm not going to sit around and justify them to someone who has never had to make any hard choices in her life. It's like being up here," he said, gesturing around as he stood. "If I left you right now, you might find your way down on

61

your own. Maybe you'd even be able to get back through the desert without falling on a cactus or pissing off a rattlesnake. But while you were doing it your mind wouldn't wander to math problems or college applications. Your focus would be on survival."

The fear of him actually leaving her right now was nearly paralyzing. He was right, if she had to get back to the house on her own right now, she probably could, but it would take all her effort, there would be none left for anything else. "Your analogies are frighteningly good," she admitted. "You'd be a great writer, and my grandmother would love you."

The silence that hung there was a clear sign Tao wasn't accustomed to compliments and had no idea how to respond. In the absence of words came a noise that rattled Frankie to her core. A dozen whine-like howls echoed through the darkness, all piled on top of each other as if competing to be the loudest.

"Coyotes," Tao explained through a smile, clearly enjoying the fear that had leapt out from the night and landed on Frankie's face.

"Tao," Frankie whispered, biting at her lip as the fire sparked and flickered in front of her, "don't leave me up here, okay?"

He laughed, tossing his head back and sending his shaggy black hair flying behind him. When he glanced back, Frankie's face was serious. The coyotes let loose their song again, and she jumped, clutching at her heart.

"I won't," he assured her as he sat back down. "I wouldn't leave you here."

Chapter Eight

As the sun rose the next morning, Frankie felt the urge to pull the blanket over her head and stay in bed all day. Or on the couch all day, since that was where she was sleeping. This was to be the first real day of her life. She was supposed to be waking up in Maxwell's arms, ready to test the waters of real journalism, not the boring high school newspaper she'd been stuck working on for the last three years. Instead she was bent uncomfortably on a tiny couch facing the prospect that she might not even see Maxwell on this trip.

A few of the many locks on the front door came to life, spinning and clicking as Frankie finally sat up. Lila stepped through, looking like she'd fallen prey to a zombie apocalypse. Her eyes were rimmed with dark circles; her warm brown skin was pale. The uniform she'd left the house in had gone from crisp and pressed to wrinkled and splattered with food.

"Did I wake you?" she asked, tiptoeing into the living room apologetically.

"No, I've been awake. I still haven't adjusted to the time change I guess. I wanted to say I'm sorry if I was rude last night. Things haven't gone the way I'd hoped, and I was disappointed." Frankie rubbed her tired eyes and stretched her aching back.

With a knowing glance and a tired exhale, Lila let Frankie know she understood the feeling perfectly, which made Frankie feel stupid. How trite of her to complain about her unraveling situation when of course this wasn't the scenario she had planned for her own life either. At least when this was over for Frankie, she would still have an amazing future.

"Did Tao behave himself?" she asked, staring over at his bedroom door as though she could cut through it with her laser eyes if the answer was no.

"He was great," Frankie blurted out without enough thought. Had she really thought of him as great? Wasn't he a jerk, an arrogant, judgmental know-it-all? Or was he actually right about most of what he had said, and helpful in distracting her from being upset? *Was he great?*

The only person who looked more astonished by the revelation was his mother. "Great?" she asked disbelievingly. "Tao was great?"

Frankie laughed. "He was nice. I was kind of being a baby because my plans fell through, and he offered to help me today since Maxwell can't come out."

"Oh," she replied with an odd smile as though she knew something Frankie did not. "I see." She shook her head knowingly and Frankie searched her eyes for a clue. "Since you're in good hands I guess I'll go crash and try to get some sleep. You two are welcome to the car today, just please keep Tao out of trouble."

"Yes ma'am," Frankie assured her as she watched her walk with slumped shoulders toward her bedroom. She caught just one more mumble from the woman before she disappeared. *"Tao was great?"*

Frankie rustled through her bag and grabbed some clothes, desperately hoping for a hot shower. It was early, but she was anxious to get her day started. She had a notebook full of research and a thousand questions to try to build the framework of a powerful article. All she needed today was people to ask and hopefully not offend. She shuffled toward the shower and tossed her clothes down on the toilet, evaluating herself in the cracked vanity mirror. This day was much different than she had hoped for, but maybe she could save it. Maybe she could still accomplish something great.

After a few minutes she figured out how to get the shower on at a reasonable, if not a little cold, temperature. She slid the rickety glass door open with a hard tug and stepped in with a shiver. A cold shower wasn't her favorite way to start the day, but so far that's what this trip was about, making the best from what you were given.

She had a wave of claustrophobia rush over her as she closed the glass door. The shower was so tiny she wondered how Tao even fit in it. Then she instantly forced the vision of Tao in the shower out of her head. That was dangerous.

The walls practically touched her on every side as she lathered shampoo into her hair, another chill running down her spine. The water had to get hotter than this she thought as she fiddled with the knob, forcing it harder to the left. She was right; the water did get hotter, a *lot* hotter as the knob pulled off in her slippery hand. "No," she cried as looked down at the broken knob and felt the water temperature climbing to an intolerable level. "No," she cried out again as her skin began to burn. She had only one choice. She had to jump out and hope the knob could be fixed.

Her hand clutched the handle of the glass door as she wormed and squirmed under the growing heat, unable to escape. Tugging at the handle as hard as she could, her slippery hands met a jammed door as steam began to fill the tiny space. "Help," she screamed, hoping Shayna's mother hadn't fallen asleep yet. She dropped the knob and began tugging the door as hard as she could with both hands as her skin began to tingle in agony. "Help," she begged as she banged on the glass door harder and harder.

She heard the bathroom door slam open and a shadow fell on the other side of the glass. "It's stuck and the water is too hot," she cried, trying to keep the majority of the water off her body as she continued yanking on the glass door.

"Let go of the door," Tao said, and Frankie obeyed but felt her entire body grow hotter with embarrassment.

"No, don't open it, get your mom," she begged but shrieked as she backed up under the scorching water again.

"I'm not looking," he promised as he took hold of the door and, rather than sliding it off to the side, yanked it from its broken track. Driven by the pain and pure survival instinct, Frankie lunged out of the shower and nearly toppled to the floor, grabbing Tao's bare arm to steady herself. Did this kid ever wear a shirt, she wondered. But she was sopping wet and naked, so who was she to judge?

"Don't look," she shouted as he dropped the door and made a move to steady her, his eyes still pressed shut.

"I'm not!" he shouted back, both of them sounding angry but not really sure why. Frankie yanked a towel down from a hook and quickly wrapped herself in it.

"Okay, I'm fine now. You can go," she huffed, moving as close to the wall as she could so that there would be no more chance for contact between the two of them.

"What the hell happened?" he asked, reaching down for the knob on the shower floor and jumping back when the hot water splashed his arm. "Holy hell, that's scalding."

"I know," Frankie said, squirming around to look at her shoulders in the mirror. They were bright pink and steam was rising from them.

"You're burned," he said in a worried tone as his eyes fell on her bare shoulders and lingered.

"I'm fine," she insisted as she adjusted the towel tighter around her. She watched him reach in again, pluck the knob from the shower floor, and use it to shut the water off.

"The door sticks sometimes," he explained apologetically. "We have propane heat for the hot water, and it can get really hot if you aren't careful."

"I'm fine; you should go," she said gesturing with her chin toward the bathroom door.

"You still have shampoo in your hair," he replied, pointing up at her red locks piled high on her head and held in place with suds.

"I'll rinse it in the sink. Maybe your mom can come look at my back to see if it's okay," Frankie said, feeling the pain growing rather than subsiding.

"She's out cold by now. She takes some pills to help her sleep during the day. I can take you down to Calista; she's like a nurse here." Tao's eyes kept darting around the little bathroom nervously.

"Maybe I should," Frankie gulped as the pain mounted. "I can't wear my clothes," she sighed, looking down at her tiny tank top and bra that were sitting exposed on the toilet. She'd never wear her tight thin shirt without a bra, but the thought of putting that on right

67

now was overwhelming. "Can I borrow a T-shirt?" she asked, wincing from the pain as she moved the towel.

"Sure," he answered, darting out of the room, looking grateful for a job and a reason to leave. In a flash he was back with a shirt in his hand. "This one is from a concert I went to last year," he explained and then looked instantly like he knew how dumb he sounded.

"This is fine," Frankie said reaching for it, but stopping short as the towel rubbed on her tender skin. "Ow, damn," she croaked out as she fought the tears that were about to spill over. Tao leaned in the rest of the way to hand it to her.

"What can I do?" he asked, looking like a child begging for directions. But Frankie couldn't think of how he could help. Her back and butt were tingling with pain, electric shocks of heat pulsing through them. She just wanted to get dressed and get to that nurse for help. "Maybe some shorts too, like something loose."

"Shorts?" Tao asked looking her up and down. "You won't fit in my shorts. Why would you want them?"

"I burned my ass too, okay?" she blurted out and then laughed a little, punctuating it with a tiny cry of pain.

"Shorts," he said, trying not to laugh as he disappeared again. "Here are some of Shayna's. She has a bigger butt than you. They should be loose." He handed them over and stepped back to the doorway. "Don't tell her I said that."

"I won't," Frankie assured him as she gestured for him to leave and shut the bathroom door. When she heard it click she dropped the towel and turned her back toward the mirror so she could get a good look. The redness was getting worse and the pain was radiating, similar to a sunburn but more painful. Not very gracefully, she washed the shampoo from her hair and knotted it up with an elastic.

Gingerly sliding into the clothes, she winced and couldn't hold the tears back any longer. She felt like such an idiot. In one morning away from home she'd managed to injure herself, needed rescuing, and damaged the home she was staying in. How was she going to break a big story and put her name on the journalistic map if she couldn't even keep herself safe? Maybe she'd become a headline herself. *Out-of-town idiot burns herself in shower. Later dies of embarrassment.*

She spun the knob of the bathroom door and hobbled her way out. "It hurts," she groaned as she made her way toward the car, wiping away the tears.

"Don't cry," Tao said, pleading rather than comforting.

"I'm not crying," she lied.

"Calista will fix you up," Tao assured her, but there was a hint of fear in his eyes, like he too was in over his head. "Maybe I should wake my mom up."

"Please don't. I thought about it, and she'll call my mom and all hell will break loose. I can't deal with that right now."

Her only option was lying on her belly in the backseat of the car, which was impossibly humiliating. Every bump made the clothes on her body shift. It felt like sandpaper on rough wood.

"We're pulling in now," Tao called over his shoulder as the car slowed to a stop.

"Is this the hospital?" Frankie asked, shimmying to an upright position and looking around. All she saw was a house that didn't look much different from the one she'd just left.

"We don't have a hospital on the reservation," Tao explained as he hopped out of the car and came around to help her out. "We have a health center and then Calista treats people out of her house as well."

"Oh," Frankie said, not catching herself in time to keep the look of concern off her face.

"I can take you to the hospital. If you aren't comfortable here say so." Tao's tone was accusatory. He still saw her as judgmental. "It's a longer drive, but I'll do whatever you prefer."

"No, this is fine. I appreciate her helping me." Frankie flinched from the pain as she stood and caught herself on Tao's arm for the second time this morning. Before she could pull it away he placed his hand over hers, keeping it right where it was.

He helped her to the door and rather than knocking, just let himself right in. "Calista, are you here?" he asked as he gestured for Frankie to sit.

"I'll stand," she smiled, reminding him of the reason they were there. Sitting was not really an option.

"Tao?" A heavyset woman with chipmunk cheeks and two long brown braids flowing down either shoulder stepped into the living room. "What's going on here?" she inquired skeptically as she eyed Frankie.

"This is Frankie; she's friends with Shayna," Tao began, and Frankie could sense something was happening she didn't understand. "She's staying with us for a little while, and she got burned. Our stupid shower got too hot and the door jammed. Can you help her out?"

"Tao, you can't be serious," Calista scoffed. "She needs to go to the hospital off the reservation. I can't treat her here. Next thing you know her folks will be in here throwing a fit because I did something they don't agree with. I treat Tewapia. That's all."

"She's in pain," Tao explained, gesturing over to Frankie. Quickly changing tone and language, he began speaking assertively. Frankie had been too distracted the last time she heard him speak in this tongue to realize how beautiful it was. His mouth seemed to fill with extra vowels and his breath was more emphasized and purposeful. It was a powerful language, and he seemed to change his posture when he spoke it.

Frankie felt small in this room. She could deduce what the argument was about. Her. She was the problem in this equation, and she felt sorry for that. But watching Tao make a case for her, even though she didn't know what he was saying exactly, made her smile on the inside.

"Come on," Calista finally grunted as she switched back to English and waved at Frankie to follow her.

"I'm really sorry," Frankie offered as she stepped into the tiny makeshift exam room.

"Where are the burns?" Calista asked, still looking very annoyed. "You can go behind that curtain and put on one of the gowns, just leave the burns exposed for me to see."

Frankie obeyed, trying to balance her guilt for the intrusion with the desire to make the pain stop.

"Not too bad," Calista said when Frankie came out from behind the curtain with her exposed back and butt, tingling in pain. "Looks like first degree burns, maybe some second degree that will blister, but nothing that should give you any long-term trouble. I have a salve," Calista said and then stopped herself. "I don't know what you want to do here. I can't prescribe what they'd likely give you at a hospital, and I'm sure that's what you'd want. I have something we use here for burns that will give you twice the relief with no side effects, but it's probably not good enough for you."

"I want whatever will help me," Frankie admitted. "I'll take anything."

"This is a mixture of aloe, calendula, and honey, which acts as an antiseptic and things our people have been using for centuries. I'd tell you what they are, but then next week they'd be selling this stuff in the pharmacy for a hundred dollars a bottle. I can assure you it'll reduce the pain, but you might want to take some over-the-counter pain reliever as well. She handed Frankie a small jar and began fiddling around with something else to appear busier than she was.

"Can you put some of it on me?" Frankie asked desperately. "I don't think I can reach everywhere."

"I was trying to avoid actually administering anything. Can't you have Shayna do it?" Calista bit at the back of her pen as if to keep from saying something she'd regret.

"She's not here, she's at her aunt's house, and I don't have anyone else who can do it. Shayna's mom sleeps during the day. There's only Tao and—" Frankie pushed the jar toward Calista and pleaded with her eyes to not have to finish that sentence.

Calista let out a little laugh. "I guess I can't let that happen." She grabbed the jar, and Frankie spun around and cooed with relief as the gel began to work its magic. "You'll need to put that on once a day so try to make sure you have Shayna's mother do it before she goes to work. It should be better in a couple days; you'll just want to keep the sun and any more hot water off it. Try a cool bath or a swim in some cool water."

"Thank you so much," Frankie sighed earnestly. "That feels amazing."

"I do think Tao would have been happy to put this on for you," Calista laughed. "I've never seen him quite like this before. He's always too busy for girls."

"Oh it's not like that. I have a boyfriend. Tao was just helping me out because my plans fell through and Shayna wasn't around."

"I've known that boy his entire life," Calista explained as she handed the jar back to Frankie and pulled off her rubber gloves. "He's never been one to help someone who's not Tewapia, and I've never seen him look quite so worried about someone who doesn't live here. The way he looked at you," Calista began as her mouth curled into a meaningful smile, "the way he just fought for you was something special. If you do have a boyfriend be gentle on Tao's heart. He is a tough kid, misunderstood most of the time, but he's very loyal. If you aren't interested in him you might want to let him know sooner rather than later. He's been through a lot, he doesn't deserve to be taken advantage of."

"I wouldn't do that," Frankie defended. "Plus he might look concerned right now but the only thing we've done since I got here is disagree. He doesn't like me."

"Arguing is the language of love," Calista teased. "It's two hearts trying to find common ground by any means necessary."

"That's not, I mean I don't—" Frankie stuttered. "Thank you for the cream." She slipped back behind the curtain to shield her blood-red, embarrassed cheeks.

"You two can see yourselves out," Calista called over her shoulder as she disappeared out the door. Frankie got back into Tao's shirt and the borrowed shorts and stood for a moment behind the curtain wondering if what Calista had said was true. She pulled the shirt up to her nose and inhaled. It didn't smell at all like Maxwell's cologne. It was earthy and more like a spicy tea her mother would drink than a musky store-bought scent. It smelled different than Maxwell, but it still smelled good.

Shaking herself for the stupid act of sniffing his shirt, she focused on what mattered. This trip was about Maxwell and her starting something. If that couldn't happen then it was about her writing an article people would be interested in reading. It was not about Tao or how he smelled or how kind he was being to her. She loved Maxwell. That had been true for as long as she could remember.

When she stepped into the living room, she saw Tao's wide brown eyes waiting for answers. Calista was right; he was worried. He did care about her. That didn't mean he liked her, but it meant something.

"You good?" he asked, hopping to his feet.

"Yeah, I think so. I'm just grateful. Thanks for bringing me here. She gave me something for the burn, and it's helping already. It feels much better. Thanks."

Tao cast his eyes down as if to deflect the gratitude. "No problem," he answered quietly.

"And for helping me out of the shower, thanks for that too." Frankie locked her eyes on Tao's face, searching to see if Calista was right. Did he like her? Why should it matter if he did?

"I couldn't exactly leave you to cook like steamed vegetables." Tao glanced up, meeting her eyes now and smiling.

"But you were a gentleman about it. I really appreciate that." Frankie didn't meet his smile with her own. She didn't want to lighten the moment. She wanted him to answer in a way that told her something. In a way that mattered. Not as a joke.

"You needed help, I'm not going to take advantage of that situation. I'm just glad you're all right." Tao opened the front door and waited for her to step out.

"I guess I am." She shrugged as she walked past him. "I'm not sure. I'm not sure of anything anymore. I came out here with all these plans, and now where am I?"

"You're about to start your research for this big story of yours. I'm going to take you over to Danyia's mother. Her name is Chari Lifewater. She lives off her land and keeps to herself. I used to do some work around her trailer when she needed help. She'll be happy to see me."

"You want to do that now? Don't you have to work?" Frankie turned to face him as the sun beat down on her cheek. This heat was miserable. His body cast a shadow, blocking the hot rays from her eyes. It was a relief. He was a relief to have around she realized with a start. She might have to stop wondering if he liked her and instead wonder if she liked him.

"I don't start work until two this afternoon. I have time. You still want to do this, right? You're not giving up, are you?"

"No," Frankie cut back quickly. "I want to do this. I just don't understand why you want to help me."

"I have my own motives." Tao grinned.

"Oh? And what are those?" Frankie felt her stomach do a flip as she waited to hear what he had to say. Would he admit he wanted to spend more time with her? Why did she want him to admit that?

"You'll have to wait and see."

Chapter Nine

The drive to Cheri Lifewater's house gave Frankie an opportunity to get a good look at the reservation. The desert was sparse but at the same time so full; she couldn't grasp this strange paradox. The reservation itself was not densely populated, and the houses and buildings were no more than two stories high. With the land so flat and expansive, if not for the mountains that framed the valley, you'd think this place would go on forever.

Like straight-backed soldiers there was cactus after cactus standing watch on the quiet land. Twiggy bushes punctuated the landscape every few feet, battered and worn like they'd fought hard for that spot in the earth. Every glimpse Frankie had of the wildlife told its own story. From prairie dogs to lizards, they all had one thing in common. They scurried, rushing off to some safer and cooler destination. There was an urgency to the desert in the summer, a hurried pace that seemed fueled by self-preservation. As Frankie felt drips of sweat streaming down her back, she could understand why.

"You remember everything I told you about dealing with the Tewapia people, right?" Tao asked, looking like he might have changed his mind about all of this.

"Yes," Frankie assured him. "I promise I will be very respectful. There isn't much to pry about really. The story I'm trying to break is that the newspaper had or still has, a culture of bias against the reservation. I'd love to use Danyia's case as an example, but she doesn't need to tell me much. Everything is a matter of public record; I just want to build in perspective."

Tao nodded, though he still seemed unconvinced. "She's a little batty," he choked out. "Sweet and all but after her daughter died, she lost it. Chari was a champion of the Tewapia people and culture. She believed it was possible for us to restore our way of life, our language, and our beliefs. Of anyone on the reservation, she knows the most about tribal roots, and she has passed the knowledge down to many others. Spending time with her is the reason I feel the way I do about being true to my heritage. She taught my mother the language, who, in turn, taught it to me. So in a way I only have the ability because of her. If Danyia hadn't been murdered, many believe Chari would have succeeded in bringing back many of our old ways. But you'll see that's not her focus anymore."

"Do people want the old ways to come back? I would think they'd welcome changes that moved the tribe forward. At least in some ways. Look at the reservations who house casinos and stuff." Frankie had watched a few documentaries on the impact of technology on Native Americans, but she wanted to hear Tao's take on it.

"I'd welcome the old ways. It would give me some place to land. Today I feel like I have to scrape and claw to keep things alive. Most of the kids here would rather grab fast food and watch a movie than sit around and hear about the thousands of years our ancestors spent living on the land. I've learned to hunt and survive. I can sense a storm coming before anyone on the news is reporting it, and I can feel the slightest disruption in my surroundings. I wouldn't trade that for an afternoon at the mall."

"That makes sense." Frankie nodded as they approached the mustard yellow trailer that was in complete disrepair. Saying it was in the middle of

78

nowhere would not be overstating it. It sat smack dab in the middle of nothing.

"Chari, it's Tao," he called through the ripped screen door. He looked down at Frankie one more time as if assessing her readiness. It was unsettling, and she could sense the pressure weighing on her shoulders.

"Come on in." A tiny voice snaked its way through the door. The warm edges of the words made Frankie feel a little more at ease. How could someone so soft-spoken be intimidating?

When Tao swung the screen door open the top hinge came undone, and he steadied it with his hand as he gestured for Frankie to go ahead of him. She nearly gasped but settled her face just in time to greet the woman in the corner of the trailer. The smell was enough to make her nose wish it had never existed, and the stacks and stacks of magazines looked like they could topple over in an avalanche at any moment. *Hoarder.* Frankie had heard the word before, but she'd never seen it up close.

"Hello ma'am." Frankie smiled and focused solely on the woman so as not to stare at the mess. "Thank you for inviting us in."

The woman's curly hair looked like the perfect resting spot for a flock of birds. It clearly hadn't seen a brush, maybe not even a shower, for a long time. Her pointy features were draped in baggy, tired skin. She was a shock to look at, more like an extension of the messy trailer than an actual person.

"I'd never turn Tao away, he's my savior," Chari cooed, shining a bright smile at Tao who dropped his head and brushed off the compliment.

"I'll come by tomorrow and fix that door."

"Of course you will," Chari said, as she clasped her hands tightly, sending her many bangle bracelets colliding together. "Now what brings you here today?"

Frankie opened her mouth to speak, but Tao gently waved her off and cut in. "Frankie is Shayna's friend. She's here visiting, and she wants to be a journalist, someone who gives a voice to people."

Frankie felt a warm jolt blow through her chest. That was exactly what she wanted to do, but to hear Tao explain it to someone made the butterflies in her stomach erupt. He'd been able to sum her up in a few words after only knowing her a day.

"That's good, sweetheart," Chari beamed over at Frankie who was still trying to keep her knees from wobbling as she watched Tao continue to explain.

"Shayna told her about some of the problems we have here, and she wants to know more. I think she could do a great job writing about it."

"Which problems?" Chari asked, raising a hand for Tao to be silent, turning her attention to Frankie.

"Ma'am, I think there is journalistic partiality in this area. The reservation doesn't have their own media outlets or newspapers, and I think there is a culture of bias and misinformation off the reservation." Frankie felt the frog in her throat hop away as she delivered her message with confidence. She believed in this. She knew these folks were not being given fair opportunities in media, and she wanted to draw attention to it.

"Why don't you just write an article called *the sky is blue*," Chari asked, furrowing her brows. "That's not really an exposé of something no one knows about."

"Oh," Frankie replied, clearing her throat nervously and looking over at Tao for help. "I thought maybe trying to get some more attention on the issue might help."

"The sky is blue," Chari shrugged. "I suppose there are some folks who haven't noticed it, but I'm guessing that's a pretty small percentage. Blind folks maybe. Babies. Not much of an audience."

"I didn't realize that," Frankie said, biting at her lip. "When Shayna talked to me about it, I just assumed it was something that needed voiced. She told me about your daughter and how that case was handled. I thought the bias was systemic and—" Frankie knew the risk she was taking by bringing up Chari's daughter but risk was often what journalism was all about. Chari sat up straighter in her chair as she cut into Frankie's words.

"So you know then," her words running together, "you know my daughter was murdered, and no one gave a damn. Her spirit has been trapped in a turbulent no man's land for the last seventeen years. That's the systemic problem."

"Chari," Tao began, but she again raised a hand to silence him, and it worked.

"You want to give voice to our people? Give one to my daughter. Give me peace. Forget how they reported the crime. Forget how they portrayed us and focus on how they made no effort to find her body because they don't understand the torture our people go through when a person leaves this earth without the right rituals performed. Forget what they print, and pay attention to what they left undone."

"I intended to use your daughter's case as an example of the problem. I came here today to better understand how you felt about the way it was handled and how it was covered." Frankie felt they were saying the same things, but Chari's tone and expression showed she didn't agree.

"Your ears are not connected to your heart," Chari interjected, standing and grabbing Frankie by the arm. "Come with me." She pulled Frankie through the broken door and behind the trailer to a small teepee. "Go," she insisted, and Frankie complied, climbing in the tiny space. "It's time to connect."

Frankie stayed silent, hoping Tao would join them as Chari lit incense sticks all around them, clouding the small space with a variety of savory and woody scents.

"I am the mother of a child who was murdered," Chari said as she ran her fingers over Frankie's eyes to close them. "My child's spirit is damned to a purgatory of the lost until her body is brought to me to be blessed and cleansed. I don't know what happened to her. I don't know where she is. I only know she is suffering and, in turn, I suffer. And no one who has power to help me understands or cares about that. Instead they go out of their way to protect their own, pushing me farther from the truth. They hide away the one person who knows what happened and claim he is dead. What do I care about?" Chari asked, touching Frankie's arm. "What do I care about?" she repeated as Frankie opened her eyes.

"Finding your daughter's body," Frankie whispered.

"I don't care what they wrote in the paper. I don't care what story they tell. I want my child to rest peacefully. I want someone who can help."

"Maybe if I get the dialogue started with my article—" Frankie offered but stopped short when Chari shook her head.

"Why are you here?" Chari asked. "You are a young girl; why bother yourself with this?" Her eyes narrowed as though she were peering right into Frankie's heart. She could sense something more was going on, and she wouldn't stop prying until she knew what it was. So Frankie gave what she was looking for.

"I want to be a good journalist. My career is supposed to mean something, and I want it to start right now." Frankie raised her eyes to the small opening at the top of the teepee and begged the tears not to fall, but they betrayed her. "I have this plan. Sitting around and waiting isn't acceptable. I'm ready for life to start. I'm going to make it start . . . now."

Chari nodded her head in complete understanding. "And that's working?"

"Not even a little bit. It's falling apart. I thought I knew what I was coming out here to do, and in five minutes, I realize how wrong I was. I thought I'd be doing this great thing, and it turns out it doesn't even need to be done. My interesting story won't really interest anyone. My parents are so hurt, and what did I do that for? I had a plan, but none of it has turned out. So I did all this damage for nothing. I'm sorry if I've insulted you by coming here. I wanted to help and prove something to myself, to everyone."

"People who are too driven push away all the good to get to where they think they want to go. Most times it doesn't turn out to be what they wanted at all. And then they find out there is no one left to share the sadness."

"But I've had this in my mind for so long. All of this—moving here, being a big-shot journalist who makes my own success. What am I supposed to do now?" She dropped her face into her hands and cried.

"Do something that matters," Chari whispered. "Don't do it alone. Don't do it by burning bridges behind you. Do great things so you can still go back when you're done. You can do good without hurting people you love."

"What can I do?" Frankie asked, peeking out from behind her fingers. "What is left for me?"

"What do I care about?" Chari chanted again.

"Finding your daughter's body," Frankie answered, but she still couldn't connect all of this. What could she possibly do to help that cause? It had been seventeen years, and the police hadn't found her; what could Frankie do? "I don't know how to do that."

"I don't either," Chari shrugged, her eyes looking distant now. "But no one has tried before. No one has listened. No one has cared."

"I care," Frankie promised, reaching her hand out and touching Chari's bracelet-covered wrist.

"Then help," Chari said as though it was the simplest idea in the world. "Just help me."

Chapter Ten

"I don't understand," Tao said after a long period of silence on the ride back toward his house. "She wants you to find Danyia's body?"

"She wants me to help. I thought I knew what was important. I was dumb enough to assume I understood the point of all of this, but it's not about how people reported this story. Chari just wants peace. She deserves that."

"Great," Tao laughed. "So you're going to change gears and solve a cold murder case? That sounds easy."

"I don't know, Tao, okay?" Frankie said, tossing her hands up in the air in defeat. "I have no idea what I'm going to do. All I know is this trip just keeps being one big kick in the stomach. This was supposed to be me starting my life. Maxwell and I were going to find the apartment we'd live in. Now he won't answer my text messages. I was going to write this powerful piece about injustice and bias. My parents would see me for what I really am, an adult who is ready for independence. Instead I broke their hearts and have nothing to show for it. The story I thought would be so captivating is old news. What the hell am I supposed to do? Who am I? I'm failing, and I'm hurting people. And *I'm* hurting; this hurts." Like a derailed train, Frankie's words piled up on each other, crashing together.

Tao pulled the car over to the side of the long stretch of road and put it in park. "Why do you do this to yourself? Who said you had to have life all figured out by now? Cut yourself some slack."

"That's easy for you to say; no one expects anything out of you. You can drop out of school, and that's fine with everyone. I have these people who have been reminding me my whole life that I have a purpose, that I can be something great. I'm surrounded by people who make a difference." Frankie couldn't see past her own pain to realize the direct hit her words had just delivered.

"You need a wake-up call," Tao barked back. "You know why *everyone* isn't up in arms about me quitting school? Because my *everyone* is my mother. My dad drank himself to death when I was still in diapers. I don't have aunts and uncles cheering me on. I have two people who depend on me. If I go back to school next year I won't be able to take the full-time position that's opening at the gas station when Tim retires. He's been pumping gas for forty years, and my best bet at a future with any kind of security is to do the same. I have to step right into his footsteps as he leaves. My mom can't work forever. She needs to know when she can't go on anymore I'll be there to help Shayna. I'm sorry the pretend weight of people's expectations is heavy for you to carry, but try some real expectations and see how that feels. When your paycheck keeps the lights on in your house or pays your sister's way to SAT prep classes then you can talk to me. Everything is yours for the taking. Stop complaining about how your fairy tale isn't panning out and start dealing with real life. If this guy is too much of a selfish jerk to make time for you, why change your whole life just to be with him? You deserve better than that."

Frankie swallowed back her defense of Maxwell. Tao didn't know him like she did. He couldn't possibly understand what this internship meant for Maxwell and why he couldn't be here. But there was plenty he'd said that was true.

"I didn't realize that's why you weren't going back to school," Frankie offered back, but she could tell it was too late for a simple apology. "You can drop me off at your house."

"No," Tao sniped. "What are you going to do? Things aren't going your way. Things aren't what you thought, now what?"

"I don't know." Frankie shrugged. "Maybe I should grab a bus and go see Maxwell. Maybe if I see him I'll feel better. I could get his opinion."

"He can't even make time to call you back; you think he's going to drop everything just because you show up? This isn't as important to him; you have to face that."

"What do you do when you feel like everything is falling apart?" Frankie asked, realizing he likely had to face moments like this. This wobbly tightrope she found herself on was where he spent most of his time. The difference was she had a net held by people ready to catch her, but Tao was doing most of his alone.

"You sure you want to find out? Yesterday you had me pegged as a kid running into the woods to do keg stands with his buddies around a fire." Tao sent her a sideways glance that felt like a dare.

"Well, there was a fire involved. But I misjudged you." Frankie shrugged. Don't feel too special, apparently I've misjudged a lot of stuff lately."

"So now you trust me?" Tao asked with a victorious grin, already anticipating the answer.

"You've been pretty good to me so far," Frankie admitted. "And everyone we've met seems to like you. Not to mention my only other plan is going back to your house, pulling the covers over my head, and crying. Whatever you have planned has to be better than that."

"It will be. And we can make a stop on the way. There's something I want to get from the library." Tao slowed the car and turned it around, sending them back in the other direction.

"Won't you be late for work?" Frankie asked, looking concerned.

"We've got hours. We'll be fine. This will be worth it."

Chapter Eleven

This girl. This uptight, dramatic, know-it-all girl had gotten in his head and somehow managed to stay there. Like a tick buried in his skin, she took hold. Tao had been up late last night staring at his ceiling, wondering what Frankie was doing on his couch. Was she asleep? Was she still upset? Did she want to talk? He'd punctuated each of those thoughts with a firm, *who gives a damn?*

But the answer was clear. He did. From the second he'd walked into the living room and saw her there with her bag slung over her shoulder and her lips in a pout, he couldn't get her out of his head. He'd been so prepared to hate her. This was the little white rich girl his sister worshiped because their family had tossed a few gracious bones her way. This was the snob who traveled the country and got everything she wanted from her daddy. He latched onto that idea like a young man clinging to the edge of a cliff, hanging by his fingertips with all his might. But little by little she'd lifted one finger at a time until he finally had no choice but to let go. She wasn't entitled; she was kind. She wasn't blowing her nose with hundred dollar bills; she actually seemed to live pretty modestly according to the way she talked about home. And worst of all, she was beautiful. Her eyes were like sea glass; her hair was bright red, something Tao had never seen before. She had cute little freckles dotting her nose and long fluttering lashes. He found himself staring, examining her tiniest features so he could commit them to memory. Damn it.

Growing up in a house with women, he was susceptible to the power of tears, and Frankie's had proven no different. Her aching heart tugged at his own and in those moments he felt like he could flip the world upside down just to make her feel better.

Now, as he watched her eyes grow wider with each hairpin turn they took up the mountain, he felt like a king. Her hand was clutched tightly to the center console, and it took all his effort not to reach out and hold it.

"These roads are insane," she sputtered as they took another sharp turn that put the car a few feet from the edge of a cliff.

"I know them well," Tao assured her. "Don't worry."

"I've been up mountains back home but nothing like this. Where are the guard rails and the safety signs?" She sucked in a sharp breath as they crested a hill and banked hard to the right. Her hand jumped and slapped to his shoulder. "This is crazy," she said, but the smile on her face was so wide he knew she was dancing between fear and excitement.

"Wait until you see it." He smiled back, knowing every worry she had, every pang of disappointment she was feeling, was about to be swallowed up. This magic had always worked on him, and he knew it would do the same for her.

"See what?" she asked, her eyes looking half worried and half thrilled.

"There," he answered as he pointed to their left, the whole world opening up before them. Killan Lake was an untouched, majestic slice of heaven. Cutting its way through a vast canyon of red and orange rock, it stood before them like an oasis.

"That is absolutely . . ." Frankie paused, unable to find a word to describe the view in front of her. Tao parked the car as his body buzzed with the excitement of sharing this experience with someone else.

"I know," Tao agreed, not needing to hear her finish the sentence. "But it gets even better. The car rested in a dirt inlet over the water, and he hopped out, gesturing for her to hurry up and do the same. She jumped out and then looked as though she regretted it as she winced in pain.

"This stupid burn," she groaned, wiggling uncomfortably in the T-shirt he'd given her earlier that morning. Nothing had ever looked better on anyone in the history of clothing.

"You'll forget all about it in a minute. You'll forget all about everything. Just follow me." He waited until she was right on his heels before descending the steep, rocky embankment toward the water. He'd spent his whole life steadying his feet over rough terrain and learning how to move when the earth moved beneath him. This was easy for him, but he knew she might be a little less sure-footed. When her hands clamped his shoulders he felt a shock jolt through his body. "You good?" he asked, turning halfway to see her.

"I'm fine. Just don't fall because we'll both end up on our asses."

"I've got you," he promised as he navigated them closer to the edge of the water where the brush grew thicker. "Be careful here, you don't want to brush against that cactus. I'm not sure Calista will patch you up twice in one day."

"We aren't going to swim, are we? We don't have a change of clothes, and I hate to dash your hopes, but I'm not skinny-dipping."

Tao blocked his mind from that thought and focused instead on the job at hand. "Nope, not skinny-dipping. We're rafting."

He'd spent an entire summer gathering the materials from the woods and building the raft, using the techniques he'd read about in books about Tewapia craftsmanship. He pulled the raft from the bank and shoved it into the water.

"We're going to get on that?" Frankie asked, and Tao took pleasure in the look of unease growing on her face.

"This type of raft held full families for generations; it can deal with your skinny ass. Just hop on." He held it steady with one arm and extended his other to help her. With an unconvinced glare, she took his hand and tumbled ungracefully onto the raft. Snatching an oar from the bank before pushing off, he took in the familiar feeling of relief that always came. "Lie on your back," he instructed as the light current began to take the raft out of the small inlet and into the widest part of the lake.

"I can't." She sighed. "The burn is starting to hurt again. I think my upper back got the worst of it."

"Do you have the stuff Calista gave you?" Tao asked as he skillfully paddled away from the shoreline.

"Yeah, but I need help with it. I can't reach all of my back. It's fine though. I can just sit up."

"Unacceptable." Tao gestured for the jar of cream, and she laughed as though it was the most ridiculous suggestion she'd ever heard. "Oh please, you would rather sit in pain than have help? You're that stubborn?"

"That's not it," Frankie insisted, and the way her face bashfully turned downward made his heart skip a beat.

You don't look like that unless you feel something. Maybe she was feeling the same way he was.

"Stop." Tao kept his hand extended, unwilling to back down. "Don't make a big deal out of it. It's medical. Think of me like your crinkly faced school nurse giving you a scoliosis exam."

"Gross." She grimaced but handed over the small jar of cream and turned her back toward him.

"I'm not putting it on your butt," he said with phony seriousness. "If that's what you were trying to get me to do by burning yourself, that's pathetic."

"Just get the middle of my back where I can't reach and then shut up." She pulled up the shirt he'd let her borrow and exposed the soft skin of her back. It was dotted with a couple freckles, and the curve of her spine was fragile and delicate. The skin was still pink and hot from the burn. While his eyes roamed over her bare skin his brain forgot to tell his arms how to move.

"Tao?" Frankie asked, looking over her shoulder expectantly at him. "What's the matter? Do I have scoliosis?" she teased.

He covered his palm with the salve and swiped his hand across her back. When she recoiled he peppered her with apologies. "Not so hard," she begged as she relaxed her back again and waited for him to continue. There was something about being hurt, sad, and in pain that had a hold over him he couldn't explain. He'd always felt protective of his mom and sister but never of anyone outside his family. Not in this way.

"Thanks." She smiled at him as she pulled the shirt back down. It was like the sun setting, beautiful to watch but you were sad to see it disappear. "So why exactly do we have to lie down on our backs?"

Danielle Stewart

"When we get around this bend you'll see," Tao assured her as he settled himself down and tucked his arms behind his head. The raft was just big enough for the two of them to lie by each other, and if she didn't want to feel like she was falling off she'd have to tuck herself just below his arm. And, much to his pleasure, she did just that. As the raft drifted slowly around the bend Tao didn't look at the sight he'd come here to see, instead he watched the profile of Frankie's face change as she saw the magic happen.

On either side of them were the steep rocky walls of the canyon. They stretched so high that, from this angle as you inched by them, it looked as though they touched the sky.

"This is incredible," Frankie whispered, and he watched a tear fall from the corner of her eye and trail down to her delicate earlobe.

"Why are you crying?" he asked as he rolled to his side to get a better look at her. She stayed steadfast, staring at the rocks and the sky.

"I think I was wrong to come out here, and now I'm not sure what to do. I'm scared to admit maybe I don't know what I'm doing. How will I know I'm doing the right thing?" She raised one arm and brushed off a few more tears.

"Don't be afraid of choices, Frankie. I wish I had them. Just don't rush into anything."

"But Maxwell expects—" Frankie choked out but stopped short when Tao raised his head up on one elbow.

"He doesn't get to expect anything out of you. If he cares about you he'll wait until you figure things out." He felt a surge of anger that this guy was making Frankie feel pressured in any way.

"You don't understand things between Maxwell and me."

"Then explain them. It's only you and me out here. If you stare up like that, anything you say is going to get eaten by the sky. That's how I like to think about it."

Closing her eyes she looked as though she were picturing the sky enveloping anything she had to say and carrying it away.

"I met Maxwell when I was fourteen. From the second I saw him I knew he was different. He was like me. And it's hard when you're young to find someone who thinks the same way as you about school and a career. I felt like he understood me when no one else my age did."

"He's not your age." Tao let the words jump out but immediately regretted them. "Sorry."

"He packed his schedule so full he made it through school in three years and was ready for law school. This internship will fast-track him by making contacts and networking. He can make a name for himself already. He's amazing. I love him. But now I'm out here and away from my family, who I hurt, and I'm wondering if I'm ready for this. I was so positive, so unwilling to admit I had some doubt. Just talking about it is scary."

"Is this one of those moments where you want me to just listen, or do you want my opinion?"

"Boy, you did grow up with women, huh?" Her tiny smile lifted her profile from sad to relieved for just a moment then collapsed again. "I'd like to hear what you have to say. I'm wondering what this all looks like from the outside."

"Okay, remember you told me that. I'll admit I don't know Maxwell so I'm not judging him, just the situation.

I'm sure you wouldn't deal with a jerk so he's probably a nice guy." Saying that made Tao want to roll his eyes, but he knew there was no point in dumping on some guy she was hung up on. Frankie seemed to be a logical person so that's what he'd use to tell her what he saw. "I don't think it's fair of him to expect you to just be waiting around for him. It's like you're this toy he puts up on the shelf so whenever he wants it, it's there. But is that really what you want to be doing?"

"I plan to be working on my own stuff, too. I'm not going to be sitting around watching soap operas. I want a career, and I want school. He's just looking for me to be here to support him. Why wouldn't I want to do that?"

"I get it. He has a long night or a bad day and he gets to come home and know there's someone waiting for him who cares. That's really nice, right?"

"Exactly," Frankie agreed, nodding her head up at the clouds.

"So what happens when you have the bad day? When you fail a test or screw something up, and you want to come home and have someone there for you. Then what?"

"I-I," Frankie stuttered out. "I won't need as much support. My classes won't be like his and my job—" She stopped herself mid-sentence and cupped her hand over her mouth as though it had been someone else speaking.

"You're as important, Frankie." Tao stared at the side of her face as her eyes grew wide in disbelief.

"I can't believe I'm rationalizing things this way. I love him so much. This is what I've always wanted. But I never wanted to be the girl who minimized her own importance to make a guy feel good."

"You can love someone but not love the life you have with them. It's like me, here at the reservation. I love this place but at the same time, it's killing me. The difference is you still have choices."

"I don't," Frankie said, tears streaming down again. "I already told Maxwell we'd be renting an apartment. We have plans. He sat across from me last night and told me how much he loves me and wants to be with me. I've made him wait so long already."

"Stop," Tao called out loudly and his voice echoed through the canyon. "You don't make decisions about your life to protect someone's feelings. That never works out. You'd hurt him more in the end."

"It's not just the commitments I've made to him. I'm not ready to say all of that. It's like I'd be saying my entire life has gone back to square one. That's too scary." Frankie rolled on her side and faced him, looking for something more out of him, though he didn't know what.

"You'll be all right," he assured her, softening his face the best he could. "Everyone is scared sometimes."

"When was the last time you were scared?" Frankie asked, begging for a distraction from her pain.

He wanted to tell her he was scared right now, but it wouldn't help her confusion. If he wanted to sit around and accuse Maxwell of being selfish, he couldn't do the same thing. Instead he thought of the last wave of fear that had rolled over him. "You asked me why I sleep in the bedroom and Shayna has the living room. A couple years ago in the middle of the night a guy broke in the window of that bedroom and robbed us. Shayna was really shaken up. The guy wasn't there to hurt anyone or anything, but when someone breaks in your window in the dead of the night you get scared."

97

"What happened?" Frankie asked like she was watching a horror movie and the music had just swelled to a crescendo.

"I grabbed a bat and scared the guy off. The laws on the reservation are flawed. The Tribal Police can't do anything to him because he's not a resident. The cops off the reservation won't really come to investigate anything. So he ran off and we let him. Odds are he knew the law and drove out here because he didn't have to worry about getting in trouble. It happens more than you'd think, which is why we don't tend to roll out the welcome mat for too many people."

"I knew the Tribal Police were limited in their options for arresting people who didn't live on the reservation, but I didn't realize it was such a black hole. That is scary."

"So that's why Shayna doesn't want the bedroom anymore. I fixed the window, but she couldn't sleep. So I added some locks to the front door, and she moved her stuff to the living room." He could feel Frankie's eyes on him now as he rolled onto his back and stared up to the sky. "That's the last time I was scared."

"I'm sorry," Frankie whispered. "I'm sorry you have to be scared and be the person who gets the bat. I've always had so many people in my life to do those things for me. One time a guy behind me in the movie theater kept messing with me and saying some nasty stuff, and I texted my Uncle Bobby. You've never seen anyone get anywhere so fast in their life. I just wanted him to be there when the movie was over, so I could get to the car without any problems. He marched right into the theater in his police uniform and shined his light right in the kid's face. He said something about what he'd do to him if he didn't leave me alone. I remember the whole place turned to watch. It was epic. The funny thing was I have a ton of people on my speed dial who'd do that for me if I needed it. All I've been trying to do lately is act like I don't need it. Like it's a bad thing. I cut them out."

"They don't have to get a vote in what you do, Frankie, but I think they've probably earned an opinion. You could hear them out. Don't anticipate what you think they're going to say, listen to them."

"I really thought I had this all settled," Frankie faltered, tears falling again. "Promise me something, Tao?" she asked as she tipped her head to look at him. He stayed focused on the ever-changing clouds rolling by and nodded gently. "No matter what I pick, no matter what I decide to do, someone is going to be hurt. I'm going to disappoint people. Promise me that whatever I do, you won't give me shit. Promise you won't take sides. Maybe if I know one person isn't going to do that, then it'll be okay."

He felt her delicate fingers creep into his and squeeze down tightly. He hadn't expected her to touch him, to need him. He had spent all this time convincing himself not to do what she just did. Was it okay then? Was he still being selfish? He tried to fill each side of the scale in his mind to see how it would balance out, but her voice took him back to the moment.

"Promise?" she asked again, squeezing his hand.

"Yeah," he blurted out with a rattle in his voice. "I promise. I've got your back."

Chapter Twelve

"I almost forgot," Tao called, poking his head back in the front door. "Here's the stuff I got from the library on our way to the lake."

Frankie's head was still swimming so the stack of papers in his hand wasn't registering. He'd made her wait in the car while he'd run an errand in the library. She'd thought it was peculiar, but she hadn't asked. "What is it?"

"It's a place to start on Danyia's case. Everything that was printed in the papers, the police report, and anything else I could find. Maybe you'll find a gem in there."

"Yeah, maybe I'll solve a cold case no one else has been able to for the last seventeen years with some stuff you dug up in the library," Frankie scoffed, but she took the papers and offered back a tiny smile.

"No one has been trying to solve it." Tao nodded his head and turned back toward the yard. He had a three-mile walk ahead of him, and Frankie wished there was more she could do to thank him.

"Is that you, Frankie?" Lila asked, coming out of her bedroom like a bear after winter's hibernation.

"Yes, ma'am."

"You were gone all day? You and Tao?" Lila yawned and rubbed her neck as though it was sore.

"Yes," Frankie said. "He took me to do some research around the reservation. He was really helpful."

Lila had that familiar smirk that seemed to creep up every time Frankie talked about Tao. "Good, I'm glad to hear it. What's all that in your hands?"

"Tao got me some stuff from the library. I was thinking I would write an article about the bias in the local media against the reservation."

"Well that's old news," Lila giggled, but she stopped abruptly at the sight of Frankie's sad eyes.

"I know that now. So I'm changing gears. Maybe I'll look into the case that I was going to cite as an example and actually investigate it a little. It sounds dumb and probably won't turn into anything, but Chari Lifewater asked me to."

"You're talking about Danyia's murder?" Lila asked, dropping her hands down to her sides. "That's a hornets' nest you don't want to kick. It's admirable that you'd even consider it, but I'm not sure it's a good idea."

"Don't worry too much." Frankie laughed. "I'll never find anything of use. I feel so bad for Chari. She seems like she's tortured every day she doesn't know what happened or where her daughter is. I can't imagine that."

"It sounded like your own mom got a little glimpse of that when you came out here," Lila countered, pretending she was busy as she braided her hair skillfully in the cracked hallway mirror.

"I guess." Frankie shrugged. "That reminds me, I actually have to check in with them soon. I promised I'd do it every day."

"Good," Lila replied. "That's real good. Now don't get too caught up in that case. There were a lot of shady characters involved. That kid, the one who killed Danyia—the one they said died the day they were going to arrest him—his uncle was a cop. A loud-mouthed, angry racist jerk, who harassed any one of us he ever came across. Garrett Monroe was his name. Luckily he's dead now. His kids took their inheritance and cleared out of here as fast as they could. That's after they spent almost a year fighting over the money and how it was split. The whole family was screwed up. There won't be many people for you to even talk to about it. That's probably for the best."

"Good to know. I'm going to check in at home." Frankie grabbed her cell phone and began scrolling through the names as Lila disappeared into her room.

"By the way," Lila said, peeking out and pointing one finger in the air like she'd just remembered something. "Shayna's not coming back this weekend. Her aunt needs her a little longer. She sends her apologies, and like I said before, you are welcome to stay as long as you'd like."

Frankie settled her face, not wanting her disappointment to be misconstrued as ungratefulness. Plastering on a big smile, she nodded and gave an awkward thumbs-up.

Turning her attention to her phone, Frankie huffed. Who she'd call needed to be a calculated choice. She was feeling fragile, on the brink of changing everything. She needed to talk to someone who would listen to her heart. Clicking down on the name, she held her breath.

"Grammy," she began, praying the voice on the other end of the line would be warm like honey not sharp and angry like the last time she'd heard her.

"I had a good feeling you'd pick me to check in with. Your Aunt Piper owes me five dollars now." Betty cackled a little laugh and every butterfly in Frankie's stomach fluttered away.

"Of course I'd call you," she croaked, quickly clearing her throat to settle her rattling voice.

Like a bloodhound who'd caught a scent, she heard her grandmother moan with concern. "What is it baby girl? Did something happen?" The alarm in Betty's voice made Frankie want to cry even more.

"I'm not sure about a few things, that's all." Frankie picked at the seam of the couch where the cushion had begun to come apart.

"You seemed sure about everything yesterday," Betty said in a singsong voice to the tune of *we told you so.*

"I knew you were still mad," Frankie said, sucking in a deep breath and flopping backward onto the couch.

"Oh please child, I could join the Olympics for this. Your mother put me through more drama than a whole Broadway show. I'll admit I was feeling a little wound up yesterday until I heard your voice and was sure you were all right. But once I knew you were out there with good people and safe, I calmed right down."

Frankie could hear old familiar noises in the background, and it made her stomach twist into knots. The clock that chirped like a bird every hour was singing, and the hum of Betty's static-filled radio chimed through the phone and into her ears. "The list of good people here helping me is drying up like a well in July."

"Why's that?" Betty asked. Frankie could map her movements by the background noise. Her grandmother had just put down a baking sheet, a tinging noise reverberating as the metal touched down on the stone tabletop. Then she'd crossed the kitchen and pushed open the screen door, the telltale squeaky hinge screeching out. After that she slumped in her rocking chair, the wood settling around her body with creaks that sounded like music to Frankie's ears. She closed her eyes and pictured it all.

"It's no big deal. Maxwell was on this waiting list for an internship, and they called him to tell him he got it. I saw him for all of four hours before he left. Now he's a couple hours away and about as busy as one person could possibly be. I've texted and haven't heard a single thing from him. Shayna is stuck at her aunt's a little longer. She was supposed to be back this weekend but now she's not coming home. Her mom works third shift and sleeps during the day, so it's just me and Shayna's brother, Tao." Frankie had to pull her hand away from the mindless fiddling with the couch when the seam split open another inch.

"What's he like?" Betty asked, the rhythmic song of her rocking chair playing like background music through the phone.

"Different," Frankie shrugged, still not sure how she was supposed to describe a guy like Tao.

"Different good or different bad?" Betty asked like she was casting a line out into a lake hoping to catch something noteworthy.

"I don't know," Frankie huffed. "He's not like anyone I've met before. He's passionate about his heritage, which is interesting. He's loyal, really trying to help his family out here. I thought he was an ass yesterday when I met him, but now I don't know. He seems like a good guy. He's helping me out."

"Hmm," Betty hummed. "That sounds promising. You'll be able to get that big story going in no time I'm sure."

"Hah." Frankie faltered. "I think I should have done a little more research about it before I hopped a train and came out here. I was so caught up getting here and having my way, I forgot the most important part of journalism. Make sure whatever your writing isn't already common knowledge. Or something no one gives a crap about."

"You're batting a thousand out there," Betty retorted. It wasn't exactly the warm, comforting verbal cuddles she was hoping for.

"So anyway," Frankie sighed, "I just promised Dad I'd check in."

"Stop it," Betty exclaimed. "Don't you rush me off the phone. I can hear it in your voice; I know you well enough. You're hurting. You're scared. There's no hiding that, not from someone who knows you so well."

"Fine," Frankie acquiesced. "It sucks out here right now. This isn't what I expected or planned, and it's terrible. I'm sure everyone back home will be glad to hear that."

"You know us so well, don't you girl? We really revel in other people's misery. Sitting around the dining room table, trading stories about the ones we love and how they fail and falter, gets our juices flowing." Betty had this other tone she used for sarcasm that always made Frankie laugh. Today however, it wasn't as funny.

"I mean, Grammy, everyone told me this was a bad idea, and now I'm going to look like an idiot. I believed if I could accomplish something worth talking about, my parents would understand me better. But now I keep asking myself why did I bother coming out here."

"You're asking the wrong question, girl. Forget what got you on the train and figure out what's keeping you there. Why haven't you just come back if nothing's working out? Is it pride?"

Frankie opened her mouth to speak but closed it quickly. She gave some thought to the question. Why not go back home? Why stay now? "It's not pride, Grammy," she replied confidently. "I still feel like I could do something out here. It's different than Edenville. People are struggling. I met a woman today who has a broken heart you wouldn't believe. Something is just telling me not to leave yet. I can still do something out here, even if it's different than I thought it would be."

"You were smart calling me, weren't you?" Betty asked, the creaking of her chair stopping abruptly. "You know damn well if you said that to anyone else they'd call you a fool and tell you to get your butt home. But me," she laughed, "I hear exactly what you're saying."

"You do?" Frankie asked in astonishment. She barely understood herself right now; she hadn't expected anyone else to figure it out.

"When you were knee-high to a grasshopper, you came begging me to let you go out in the front yard with an old glass bottle so you could catch stars. You saw them fluttering around and you just had to try to get some for yourself. I opened my mouth to tell you they were just fireflies, but I thought to myself, *why would I rob her of that sweet dream she was having? How long does a child really get to believe they can catch a star in a bottle?* An hour later you came traipsing up the stairs with a jar full of those little glowing bugs. You climbed on my lap and stared at the jar, and I watched as you realized they weren't stars at all. It broke my heart to see that piece of you fall away. It's like I witnessed you grow up a little in that moment. You whispered up to me they weren't stars, as though you were breaking bad news to me. You looked me square in the eyes and said, *I guess I'll never catch a star."*

"I remember," Frankie cut in. "You told me I could keep trying to catch one. Even if I went my whole life and never did, it was the trying the counts." Frankie laughed at the thought now; the memory had been tucked away and was now playing out in her head. "That's kind of silly, Grammy. It's physically impossible to fit a star into a bottle. It was nonsense. It's chasing something that doesn't exist."

"Maybe." Betty hummed. "But at least you'd be moving. Some people go their whole lives without a purpose. Even if yours is unobtainable, it's better to have one."

"I do like having goals," Frankie said through a smile. "Even impossible ones."

"Do me a favor, will you, girl?" Betty sighed, sounding exhausted.

"Yes, ma'am."

"Keep the steering wheel pointed in that direction. Don't stay out there because you're embarrassed to come home. Don't let it be a boy, or the hope of a boy, keeping you away. If you feel you have a purpose out there, even if it seems like it's impossible, I will be in your corner."

A telltale and impossible-to-hide sniffle betrayed Frankie. "Thanks, Grammy. I've got to be honest: I'm a little rattled. How do I know when I'm making the right choice? I've always known what I wanted, what was right for me, and now it's like I can't even figure out what to do next."

"Don't you start the waterworks because I'm not going to be able to keep myself from getting on a plane, which you know I hate, and coming out there to hug you.

You're strong, girl. This crossroad, this change in your life, we all go through it. The difference is the rest of us have never known what we wanted; we're just drifting through life being taken around at your age. You, on the other hand, have been swimming with purpose; you've been kicking those legs and fighting that stream for years, all with a destination in mind. For the first time in a long time it sounds like you've stuck your head up out of that water to take a look around."

"Exactly," Frankie agreed, trying to get herself together. "I didn't expect Maxwell to get this internship. I want to be supportive of him and be happy for him, but I'm disappointed. I know I should just wait. He waited for me for long enough, right?"

"Oh, girl. I try real hard not to give advice on love, especially first loves and all that. But I will tell you one thing: waiting is not something you want to become a habit. You've got just so many breaths in your lungs, you don't want to spend too many of them anticipating something that might never be. You feel like you might have a purpose out there, so make that important. Swim toward that. If the rest of it is right the stream will take you there someday."

"You're really in my corner with this? You don't want to just see me hop the next train home and act like nothing ever happened?" Frankie needed to hear it again. It meant something that at least one voice around the table tonight would believe in her.

"You don't need me in your corner. I'm just your branch."

"I thought we were talking about streams?" Frankie asked, teasing her grandmother for her endless list of analogies and metaphors that suited every situation.

"Hush," Betty scolded. "Don't give me a hard time about my advice because you know darn well I've never steered you wrong."

"What about that purple dress with the puffy sleeves you told me to wear to the eighth grade dance?" Frankie joked, and it felt good to have familiar banter once again.

"That stupid dress. You bring it up every time. I thought it was lovely. How was I to know that puffy sleeves had gone out of style? You're the one who decided to put that crazy braid in your hair." They were both laughing now as they recalled the disastrous dance photos.

"Like I was saying," Betty continued when she composed herself, "I'm just your branch. You can perch your bird butt on me all day long and know I'm here, but it doesn't matter. If I break, you've got yourself a set of wings. Don't rely on the branch; trust the wings."

"But how do I know my wings work? How do I know I'll fly in the right direction?"

"You don't." Betty sighed. "But remember one thing, will you?" Her voice changed from playful to pleading.

"Anything," Frankie said and meant it.

"There's no real way for you to understand the hurt in your mom's heart right now. You have nothing to compare it to, and I know you didn't mean to cause it. All I ask is that you try to make that right somehow. Remember, she's my baby girl too, and I don't like seeing her in pain. Letting a child go is a terrifying process. I know you want to be a grown-up, and I know you and your mom have had your differences. Just remember the real mark of maturity is trying to understand someone even when it's easier not to. Nobody can learn from mistakes they won't admit to. You hear what I'm saying?"

"Loud and clear, Grammy," Frankie assured her as she closed her eyes and tried to push the picture of her mother's gentle face away. "I am really sorry."

"You're gonna be all right, you know that, don't you?"

"I guess if you say it, then it must be true," Frankie teased, wrapping one arm around herself and wishing it was her grandmother's.

"You know it. Now get off this phone and go figure out if that long shot can be turned into a victory."

"Grammy," Frankie said, biting at her lip, punishing it for the quiver that had taken over, "I won't let you down."

"Of course you won't because that's not possible. There is nothing you can do and nothing you can say that will ever change my love for you. You're stuck with it."

"Promise?" Frankie asked, blinking away the sadness.

"I'm hugging you from here, little girl."

Chapter Thirteen

Frankie felt the sting return to her burnt back as she stretched, trying to keep her body from giving up on her. This was the second night straight she'd had to coach herself into staying awake in the name of research. She glanced down at her phone for what felt like the hundredth time only to find she still had no new calls or text messages.

She'd told herself sending more than four text messages to Maxwell without a reply would be desperate. So it was on him now. She wasn't going to sit around and feel sorry for her—

A chirping noise broke her thought. The screen on her phone lit, and the familiar name brought her to life. A text from Maxwell. A sign of life, finally.

Hey, what a couple of days. Sorry I've been out of touch. Lots of work but so many opportunities. I'll be able to talk more on the phone over the weekend I think. xoxo

"Who's that?" Tao asked, flopping down next to her on the couch, the pungent smell of gasoline from his work clothes wafting toward her. She was tingling with anger, and the jolt of Tao's body hitting the couch made her want to scream.

"None of your business," she shot back angrily.

"So it's good news then," he joked, leaning back on the couch and tucking his hands behind his head.

"I just got my first text from Maxwell since he left. He's nice enough to tell me we might be able to talk this weekend on the phone. Which pretty much closes the door on whether or not he is coming back on Saturday."

She threw her phone down on the coffee table that was littered with papers she'd been reading and flopped backward on the couch so she was next to Tao. "Sorry I snapped at you."

"It's fine; I'll take all the heat for your jerk boyfriend."

"He's not a jerk, Tao. He's a great guy. So great that even the lawyers in this firm can see it, and they want him there constantly." Frankie shuffled papers around the table, looking for where she'd left off in her reading.

"Maybe we should just move to a new topic, since all we ever do is argue about this." Tao nudged her with his knee and smiled even though she was rolling her eyes at him.

"Is it always going to be like this?" she groaned. "All we're ever going to do is bicker at each other?"

"You make it sound like you're going to be seeing a lot of me. Before you know it you'll be on a train back home. Then even when you come back to Arizona you'll be hours away in your new apartment waiting for your boyfriend to text you."

"Oh my gosh, how do you even stand yourself sometimes? You're so cynical and miserable. Don't worry about my life, all right? I'm going to be perfectly happy. The only thing you should worry about is helping me go through this stack of papers that are turning into a whole bunch of nothing. Help me come up with some ideas. I've already researched Denver Stills, the guy who reportedly murdered Danyia and then died himself. I read through everything I can find, which isn't much. Your mom told me all Denver's kin is dead or moved out of town."

"All of them?" Tao asked, leaning forward to see her laptop screen. "These are pretty small communities. It would be strange for a whole extended family to pull up stakes and go. Maybe they went wherever Denver is."

"We have no clue if he's still alive or not. That's purely speculation at this point."

"Sorry, your honor. The point I was making is family is family. Maybe they were just waiting for the right moment to move wherever he is. Where are they now?" Tao asked, gesturing for her to look each of them up.

"I already thought of that. I went through all of their public social media accounts, and none of them have close friends who match the description and current age of Denver. Plus they all moved to different locations and don't seem to have any interaction with each other, at least online. Denver's parents moved to California when he was still a minor so he moved in with his uncle here in town. He has a couple cousins he'd have lived with then. His uncle was a cop and his name was Garrett Monroe. Your mom said it got ugly trying to settle all the inheritance and stuff. Like I said, when the cop died, they all kind of scattered. They must have been waiting around for their inheritance, hoping to get the hell out of here." Frankie clicked a few more searches into her computer and pulled up Garrett's obituary. "Your mom seems to think if anyone was orchestrating anything it would have been this Uncle Garrett guy here. It looks like he drowned on a fishing trip about five years after Denver supposedly had his fatal car accident."

"That's probably why they were all fighting. If he died unexpectedly I bet he didn't have all his crap together for who gets what." Tao's casual comment lit a fire under Frankie that sent her fingers feverishly tapping at her keyboard.

"That's brilliant! It likely had to go to probate, which means the will in question would be public record. I just need to find the probate court from the county the will was filed in, and I'll be able to pull it up if they keep their dockets online." Frankie yanked her computer from the table and placed it on her lap so she could move even faster.

"Why, what's that going to do for you?" Tao asked, and she could feel his stare homing in on the side of her face. He had this intense way of looking at her so even when she couldn't see it, she knew he was fixed on her.

"Probably nothing, but if the uncle was really involved in this then he would have helped Denver set up some kind of life after they faked his death in a car accident. If he did then maybe he left him something in the will." She bounced with excitement as the information filled her screen.

"He's not going to leave something to a kid who's supposed to be dead. He's a cop, so I doubt he'd make that mistake." Tao dismissed the idea as he hopped off the couch and headed to the kitchen. "Have you eaten? My mom isn't much of a cook, so if you haven't noticed, we don't do dinner or anything. I'm grabbing chips."

Frankie didn't answer. She was too focused now to care about nonsense like hunger. The probate court in the county listed on the obituary did have their dockets online, which meant she'd also be able to pull up the will if it was listed. "Oh my gosh, it's right here, Tao," she announced, enthusiastically pointing at her screen.

"So what? That's not going to tell you anything."

"I don't think there is going to be something left to Denver directly. But if he was given a new identity or something, it might be listed here. We have the names of all the other family members involved in the will. If there are any names we don't recognize, we can track them down and see if they match the information we have on Denver. If he's alive this could be a way to find him. If we do, maybe there's hope for finding Danyia's body."

"I want to tell you to relax and not get ahead of yourself, but it's kind of cool watching you do this. It's sort of brilliant." Tao watched her in astonishment. "How did you even think of that?"

"Well, you have your heritage, and I have mine. These are the ways of my people." She scanned the documents, mostly legal mumbo jumbo then got down to the meat of it. She felt Tao's warm breath on her cheek as he leaned over her shoulder and moved his lips as he read. She could tilt her head and plant a kiss on him before he'd have time to turn away. But why would she? She didn't want to kiss him. *Did she?*

"Right here," he said with such excitement it sent her jumping. "This plot of land out in Cowherd Hill. It's about three hours north of here and really remote. I've been there once before. He left it to a guy named Doug Chandler. Have you seen that name anywhere?"

"No, that one is new," she replied as she opened a new screen and typed in the name. "I don't see anything on him. No social media accounts under that name based out of that area."

"Maybe he's there, living off the grid."

"Tao, we should go check. We could drive out there and see for ourselves. If this guy is alive we'd be unraveling a conspiracy. It could be huge." She stared at him with a flutter in her eyes that was begging for him to agree. But he didn't.

"We can't, Frankie. My mom's car would barely make it there in one piece, and we're not really in a position to just go knocking on the door of some guy who may have killed someone. I can try to get a couple guys from the Tribal Police to call some federal contacts and check it out."

"But I want to break this story. I don't want it getting all caught up in the political crap that goes on. I need this."

"I thought you were doing this for Cheri. I thought you wanted to give her peace and help locate Danyia's body. This sounds more like you just want your name on something big. I'm not going to put our necks on the line for some notoriety for you."

"Can't I want both?" Frankie asked, feeling heat roll up her neck that had nothing to do with her burnt back.

"As long as you have your priorities straight. Now are you going to text your boyfriend back or do you want me to call him?" Tao grabbed for her phone but she snatched it away quickly.

"Why on earth would I let you call him? What would you have to say to him anyway?" Frankie narrowed her eyes at him, scanning his face.

"I'd tell him he's stupid for leaving you here to do this on your own and he doesn't know what he's missing. Watching you work this out in your mind is something he'd be lucky to see." Tao lunged for the phone again but clearly just to make her react.

"Oh please. Are you telling me if tomorrow you got this amazing opportunity to create a career path and maybe do something that could improve the rest of your life, you'd be here with me doing this?" She started the sentence thinking she was making a point and ended it realizing she was asking an important question.

"Wild horses," he smiled, staring at her confidently. "Nothing would pull me away from here. I'd see this through no matter what."

"Right, you'd give up something like that to be with me?" Another question she didn't even know she wanted answered until she asked it.

"I would stay because this matters. No one has cared enough about this to take these chances. I honestly never thought much about it myself, and I live here. You came all this way, you wanted to tell a story, and now you want to find an even deeper version of that story. I'd stay not just to be with you but because this matters, Frankie."

"You say not *just* to be with me. Can you clarify? Is the benefit in addition to being with me or in spite of having to be with me?" She leaned toward him, no more than an inch but it felt like crossing a canyon.

"The point is I'd stay. I'm never going to be the smartest guy in a room, I get that, but I'd stay. I'd help. And the fact that you'd be there would be a good reason to stick around too. If I had a girl like you in my life there would be nothing that would keep me from her. A career is just a small part of life; it's not life. You matter, Frankie." He leaned in an equal amount, and she could feel her skin tingle with anticipation. His hand came up and brushed her cheek gently, just his rough thumb on her skin.

"Tao, thanks for helping me. This is important to me. It does matter." It was like admitting out loud that Maxwell's choice did hurt, it did make her feel small and easy to leave.

"Wild horses," he whispered again, closing the distance between them as he gently cradled her face in his hand. She clutched her phone so tightly that the ringing noise was nearly snuffed out. But it was loud enough to stop time, to stop what was about to happen. She leaned back quickly, as though she were dodging a bullet.

"It's Maxwell," she pointed out as she stood and cleared her throat, answering the phone anxiously. "Hey I didn't think I'd hear from you."

"I have a few minutes, and I felt bad for not talking to you. Are you mad?" His voice was rushed, but she could hear his genuine remorse.

"No, I'm not mad. I understand how much you have going on." She turned her back on Tao, and she might as well have slapped his face.

"I've got to tell you all about this job; it's absolutely insane. It's been seventy-two hours and I think I've slept about eight, maybe nine hours total. But my adrenaline is pumping so I'm just going to power through. They've already had two guys drop out and quit, saying it's like slave driving." Maxwell was practically vibrating with excitement as he spent the next five minutes explaining every aspect of his responsibilities and how good he was doing. She got in a few words here and there to let him know she was still on the line with him.

"Things are really changing directions here," she interjected when Maxwell stopped to take a breath.

"Oh my gosh, I got three emails while we were on the phone, all of them marked urgent. This place is nuts; I love it. Okay, I've got to run, but like I said, we'll talk over the weekend. I needed to hear your voice. It gave me a nice lift for the rest of the day. You're the best, Frankie. I can't wait to tell you more."

The line went silent, and Frankie was afraid to pull the phone from her ear and find her screen dark. But she already knew it was.

"Please don't say anything, Tao," Frankie begged with her back still turned toward him. "I can hear it; I'm not dumb. I don't need you pointing it out to me." Rubbing at her temple, she tried to think about what the hell she was doing. She was just seconds away from kissing Tao. She was questioning the one relationship that always made sense, even if it had only been a daydream until this point. Maxwell was supposed to be it. He was supposed to be the rest of her life, but if he wasn't then where did that leave her?

"I'm sorry," Tao confessed as he stood and moved toward her. "It's not fair for me to bug you about this. It's a big deal. I shouldn't have almost . . ." he trailed off, not ready to admit it was nearly a kiss. "I shouldn't be getting in the middle of this. It's not fair to you."

"I really want him to care about this," Frankie gushed, stomping her foot and launching her cell phone across the room. "I needed that. I needed to hear him give a crap about me and not just his own stuff. I wanted him to give me a reason to justify what the hell I'm doing here, some hope for what it's going to be like to be living together in a few months. He couldn't give me a single thing." When Tao's hand came down on her shoulder she felt the last lingering sensation of her nearly healed burn, and it reminded her that Tao had been there. In three days she'd learned more about his character, up close and personal, than she had about Maxwell in the last three years.

"I'm not going to give you a hard time about it anymore," he promised as she spun around and dove into

119

his arms. He wasn't ready, stumbling back half a step before he realized what was happening. She turned her head so her ear was pressed on his heart, listening to the drum that led him through life. Another long beat passed before his arms finally closed in around her.

"Please stop being so nice to me," she begged half-heartedly. "It's making me question everything in my life."

"Tomorrow I promise to insult you all day. I'll put gum in your hair. When you ask me for help, I'll tell you to go to hell and call you names. And if you get stuck in the shower again, you can just melt." He spoke into her ear, through her red hair.

She laughed and cried all at once, squeezing him tightly around the waist, so grateful he was here. "I'm sorry to put you through all this. I showed up here a few days ago and every day since has been one thing after another. I'm in this weird life crisis, and you are stuck dealing with me."

"Frankie," Tao whispered, "my life already sucked. You're entertainment to pass the time." His levity was welcomed and Frankie pinched the little meat that existed behind his arm.

"Denver Stills, or Doug Chandler," she remembered, staring up at him with twinkling eyes, "might be the key to this. There's a chance he's alive and living a few hours from here. Maybe it will be nothing, or maybe it will be everything."

"That's exactly what I was thinking," Tao said, clearly not talking about the lead they'd found. "Maybe it will be nothing," he parroted back, "or maybe it will be everything."

Chapter Fourteen

The sound of an annoyed cough woke Frankie from a deep sleep. Even before she opened her eyes, she realized she was drooling on Tao's chest. She wiped at her mouth and rubbed her eyes.

"I made a commitment to your parents to give you some distance between you and your boyfriend while you settled things with them," Lila scolded through exhaustion. "I didn't expect I'd do such a good job." She looked between Frankie and Tao as though she were waiting for some kind of an explanation.

"It's not what it looks like, Mom," Tao explained, stretching his back. "It's nothing like that. We were just up late working on some research stuff."

"Sure," Lila scoffed. "I'm supposed to believe that after the way you two have been looking at each other the last couple days?"

"Really," Frankie pleaded. "Nothing happened. We just fell asleep. We found some really promising stuff on the guy who killed Danyia, and we were putting all the pieces together. I guess we dozed off."

"What do you mean you found stuff on that guy? I told you it's not something you want to get involved with. It's not your concern." Lila didn't say the words directly, but it seemed she wanted to know what the hell Frankie was doing here.

"You're tired, Mom," Tao suggested as he stood and took the bags from her hands. He planted a kiss on her cheek and gave her a look he must have been saving up for some time. And it worked. "Frankie is really good at this stuff. I'm learning a lot sitting with her."

Lila rolled her eyes and yawned. "Just don't make a liar out of me please. I'm sure your parents don't have an objection to Maxwell specifically, it's more they want time to sort things out with you before you're here with a guy. I think they'd count Tao, too."

"Yes, ma'am," Frankie said, nodding in agreement. Tao took the bags into the kitchen and chatted with his mom before she stumbled her way into her bedroom.

"I have an early shift today," Tao said apologetically. "But the good news is there are a few Tribal officers who will be by to fuel up, and I can mention all this to them."

Frankie groaned, still not liking that plan. "Patience is a virtue I wasn't born with. What if they aren't interested in this?"

"Clearly," he laughed. "But trust me, if they aren't we'll find someone who is."

"Are you taking the car to work today?" Frankie asked, wondering if she'd be stuck at the house all day.

"No, I like walking. You can use the car if you need it."

Frankie felt relieved for the freedom. "I might go to the library to see if I can find any public records on the utilities for that property we think Denver is in. Maybe it was abandoned or rarely used before his reported death, and suddenly the electric bill was switched on. That would be another solid lead."

"Wow." Tao looked impressed. "You better only use your powers for good. You're like one toxic spill of radioactive material from being a supervillain."

In usual guy fashion, Tao was out the door to work in less than fifteen minutes, and Frankie felt the loneliness creep in. Quiet wasn't her friend right now, because her brain became a captive audience to the "what if" game. And that was a game with no winner.

She busied herself making a bowl of cereal and flipping through her notes. They'd found very little information on Doug Chandler, the recipient of the property in the will. She hadn't decided if his lack of a paper trail over the years helped or hurt her case, proving he might actually be the man who killed Danyia. It was still a long shot, but at least she was chasing something.

When her phone rang, just like every time in the last few days, she hoped it was Maxwell. There was still a part of her that was not convinced Maxwell was in the wrong. Maybe she was being unsupportive and fickle. What kind of girlfriend can't deal with some changing priorities when a career is involved? But the call wasn't from Maxwell. It was her father's office line. *That was strange.*

"Dad?" Frankie asked, feeling a knot in her stomach signaling something was wrong. Was everyone all right, she wondered? Did someone get hurt?

"Frankie, against my better judgment I'm going to give you the opportunity to explain." His voice was as sharp and hard as the metal of a samurai sword. She got hot all over and held her breath. There was something terrifying when parents got angry and you didn't know why. It made her wonder what she'd done that maybe she'd forgotten. *Did I rob a bank? Did I crash the car? No.*

"O-k-a-y," she strung out the word, over enunciating it for effect to let him know she was in the dark still.

"I'm at work right now, and I get this strange phone call from the dean of admissions at Arizona State

University. Apparently he couldn't find the right contact number for you so he tracked me down."

That was it. She felt like she was diving off the side of the Grand Canyon. Every muscle in her body tightened; she was sure they were cracking into little pieces. "I can explain," she stuttered out, even though, technically, she couldn't.

"Is the explanation that for the last few months you've been completely lying to your mother and me so you could go to the same school as Maxwell? Or, is it you've been filling out scholarship documents and writing essays for a school your mother and I haven't even thought about you going to? Because if that's the explanation—"

Frankie felt the need to fight back. "Kids go off to college, Dad. It happens every fall, and not all parents like it, but that's just the way it is."

"Don't you dare," he barked back, and she couldn't recall a time in her life when she'd ever heard him sound so angry. "This is not about you going away to college. You know we would have gone through this process with you and helped you figure out the right fit for you no matter where it was. You cut us out of that as if everything we've done over the last eighteen years doesn't matter. You had us believing this trip of yours was just some small thing, and everything would be back on track when you got home. We don't even get a voice in this. I think we've been pretty damn good to you," Michael ranted.

"You have, Dad," Frankie cried, feeling like she might throw up.

"Really? Because the first chance you get to cut us out of your life, you take it. I was trying to get my head around you being there right now. I chalked it up to some pre-college jitters or maybe some rebellious streak you needed to get out of your system. You and I are so much alike, and I knew what you were doing is something I would do. But this: applying for school out of state without so much as talking to us about it, just to be with someone you think you love. That is not something I would do."

"You have to understand. Maxwell and I have always respected what you wanted. We've never broken your rules. But now I feel like it's my time to do what's right for me. We are going to get a good, safe apartment, and I promise that I've given it all a lot of thought."

"An apartment," he choked out, sounding like she'd just confessed to murder. "You and Maxwell are going to get an apartment and go to college together on the other side of the country? You're eighteen years old and going to live with your boyfriend?" His sudden silence was more frightening than anything he'd said so far.

"I know that Mom—" Frankie started but she stopped abruptly when he began shouting again.

"No, you don't know anything about your mom. I called her, and she's devastated. I'd finally got her feeling better about this little trip you took and now this. She doesn't deserve this from you. We deserve transparency and honesty from you. That's how we've always operated."

"You weren't supposed to find out like this. After everything was settled here Maxwell and I were going to come back to Edenville together and talk to you both about it. I was going to tell you everything we had planned."

"How nice of you to come *tell* us. God forbid you ask us our opinion or feelings on any of it. You know what? Since you seem to have this all figured out, let's just move forward."

"What do you mean?" she asked, not liking how calm her father had suddenly become.

"There's really no point in you coming back here since we now know what you have planned for your life. I don't want to argue with you because clearly you have it figured out. So stay there." His voice was flat and unemotional.

"Of course I'm coming back, Dad. I told you already I'd only be out here a few weeks. I'm going to be home for the summer. That was important to Mom, right?"

"Frankie," he sighed, "I'll ship your stuff out there. I'd suggest you contact the dean of admissions as soon as possible to make sure your scholarship paperwork is all in order."

"You don't mean that, Dad. You're just angry. I'm going to come home, and we can talk about this. I think if you hear me out and understand why I did this . . ." She was pleading now, her voice crackling like dry wood in a fire.

"We're not going to agree. Let's move forward. I'm not going to have you home all summer so your mom can think she has a chance at changing your mind. I'm not going to have everyone here begging you and working to convince you of something that's clearly pointless. You have your plan and your big ideas, and we're not going to try to stop you."

"Dad, you don't understand." Frankie felt herself getting lightheaded. When this conversation started she felt a little pang of relief. Maybe her dad would demand

126

she come home right this instant. He'd take the impossibly hard choice out of her hands, and she'd be shielded behind his mandate. But instead he did the opposite. Rather than rescue her by forcing her hand, he left her stranded.

"Let me know when you have an address to send your things to." The line went silent and, like a fish plucked from the water, her mouth opened and closed, pitifully trying to gasp for air. Her father was no longer on the line.

Chapter Fifteen

Frankie grabbed the car keys and slipped her bag over her shoulder. She wasn't sure exactly where she was going, but she knew if she stayed here her sobs would draw Lila's attention, and that was the last thing she wanted right now. Her eyes were so blurred by tears that keeping the car on the road was a chore. She saw the gas station's glowing orange sign and thought of Tao. He would know what to do. He would know how to make her feel better.

Pulling in and slamming the car into park, she tilted the rearview mirror down and tried to clean her face the best she could. But there was no hiding the pain of sad, red eyes that had been wiped too many times.

"What's the matter?" Tao asked, shoving aside the cart he was using to stock the shelves and rushing over to her.

"My dad," she choked out. "He just called me because he knows about my scholarship to Arizona State."

"Oh damn." Tao gulped. "Is he coming out here or something?"

"No," Frankie said, bursting into tears. "He doesn't want me to come home for the rest of the summer. He's shipping my stuff out here. I'm supposed to stay here, get the apartment with Maxwell, and do what I want."

"Is that what you want?" Tao asked, scrutinizing her features, trying to ensure she was being honest with him.

"I-I," she argued with herself, "I don't know. I mean when I was applying for school and doing all this stuff, it's what I wanted. It's all I wanted. So much that I didn't care about what it would look like when they finally found out. But not anymore. I care how they feel. You should have heard him, Tao. He wasn't even pissed off. He was *hurt*. I hurt him after all he's done for me. You don't understand. He used to bend his entire schedule around what I needed for school. He and I used to do everything together. We had these jokes no one else knew. And he let me get away with a lot of stuff without telling my mom. And then suddenly he bails on me?"

"I don't know if I'd say he bailed on you," Tao countered as he headed behind the counter to take some cash from a customer for a pack of cigarettes.

"He just told me not to come home. Who does that to their kid? What if I were in trouble out here? What if I wanted to go home?" Frankie paced around the small gas station, flailing her arms around angrily.

"Call him back. Tell him you're not sure what you want to do, and you're sorry for how all of it went down. Go home." Tao closed the cash register with a bang and came back around the counter where she was.

"You want me to go home?" Frankie asked, a spasm of sadness hitting her. She had thought when she left Tao might have some feelings about that, but now he seemed perfectly fine to let her go, encouraging it actually.

"Please stop caring what everyone else wants. You are at the crossroad between starting college and moving in with Maxwell, or going back home and working things out with your family. Choose what feels right to you. That's what matters. But choose because if you don't you're going to realize everyone stopped waiting for you to make up your mind."

"Fine," Frankie snapped, feeling slighted by Tao's sudden indifference to what she had to do. "I'll grab a cab and go to Maxwell's hotel near the university. If my dad is trying to prove a point, that's on him. I came out here to get what I wanted, so now there is nothing stopping me. Right? No reason to stay here is there?" She waited for him to chime in, but he didn't. "Maxwell and I will do what we want."

Tao huffed loudly and rolled his eyes. "Your dad is pissed you made this decision to plan the rest of your life without talking to the people who kept you alive for the last eighteen years. You sound like a spoiled brat. I think if you put your pride aside for two seconds and forget what it will feel like to admit you were wrong, you'll get it."

"Go to hell," Frankie asserted as she flashed her middle finger in his direction. "You said you'd have my back. You promised." With a clinking of the old bell over the gas station door, Frankie bolted out. She had no idea where she was going, but she knew she was getting the hell out of there. Planting the car keys on the hood of the car for Tao, she headed off down the road in a run.

"Frankie," Tao yelled, but she didn't turn around. "There is no one here to watch the gas station. I can't go after you. I can't leave work. Come back, please."

She devoured his words, fueling her feet move faster. It was blazing hot, and she had nothing with her but her bag of clothes. Wandering the desert was a death wish. She just needed . . . what did she need? What the hell was she doing?

"Maxwell," she whispered at the cloudless blue sky. She grabbed her cell and dialed his number only to find it went straight to voicemail. Not even a ring or two to give her some hope. She needed to get to him. She needed to see him and remember how he made her feel. If she could be in his arms she'd be able to put aside the anger and hurt she was feeling.

A mile down the road she came across a pay phone with the number for a taxi company on it. Dialing the number, she planned it all out. She needed to get to Maxwell. Then everything would be fine.

Chapter Sixteen

A two-hour cab ride cost Frankie over a hundred fifty dollars, but it had been worth it. Or at least it would be once she got hold of Maxwell and told him everything that had happened. She was sitting in the library of the university because she knew she wouldn't get kicked out of there for loitering. So far she'd called him six times, but he hadn't answered. A few vague text messages about needing to talk to him hadn't worked either.

Nineteen minutes ago she had sent the real test. *Maxwell, it's an emergency; please call me right away.* If that wasn't enough to get him to stop what he was doing and pick up the phone then nothing was.

And apparently nothing was. An hour ticked by before Frankie hit a wall of reality. She had no place to sleep tonight if she couldn't reach Maxwell. She wasn't sure what hotel he was staying in. The tough thing about being an adult was eighteen didn't get you quite as much as one might think. She couldn't rent a car or a hotel room. She had enough money to get a cab back to the reservation, but that wasn't what she wanted. She was about to drop her head on the table in front of her and admit defeat when her cell phone vibrated. Making her way outside she answered in a winded and beat up kind of way, "Maxwell."

"Frankie what happened? What's the emergency?" That was the tone she needed to hear. He was frazzled and concerned.

"My parents found out about my scholarship to Arizona State. My dad is furious. He told me not to come home. As in he's shipping my stuff out here. I can't even believe he's doing this." She clenched her fist and gritted her teeth as she recounted her father's jerk move.

"This is not an emergency," Maxwell whispered. "I'm standing in a broom closet because personal phone calls are frowned upon here. I thought something serious happened. You can't do this kind of stuff."

"Something serious did happen. My parents kicked me out of the state of North Carolina. I'm here at the university and need you to come get me. I'm falling apart, Maxwell, and I need you. If you could have heard my dad."

"Frankie," he said as though he were waking her from a bad dream, "I can hear you're upset and I'm sorry, but I'm not getting out of here for another eight or nine hours."

"Then give me the information for your hotel, and I'll go there to wait for you." Frankie didn't appreciate the annoyance growing in his voice.

"You can't do that. These hotel rooms are provided by the firm, and I share mine with two other interns. We signed a contract, including not allowing anyone else to stay with us. I don't think Tanya and Mike would cover for me since we're pretty much in competition." Maxwell's voice was a raspy and frustrated whisper now.

"You're sharing a hotel room with a girl named Tanya?" Frankie asked, closing her eyes and trying not to boil over in anger.

"Please don't," Maxwell demanded. "You're sounding like a little kid now. I have no interest in Tanya whatsoever. You have to start looking at all of this differently. If this is going to work, you need to understand I'm going to need to do things you won't always like."

"Come get me, Maxwell," Frankie pleaded. "Tell them you have an emergency, and come get me."

"It'll be my last day here if I do that," Maxwell explained. "You can get through this. Just give me two minutes, and I'll call you back." The line cut off and Frankie stood for a moment calling Maxwell's name, unable to believe he'd let her go so abruptly.

Two minutes ticked by, then ten, and finally his name was flashing on her phone again. "Frankie, I've got it all worked out," he explained, and she felt the elephant on her chest stand up and walk away. "I called Shayna's mom, and she said Tao will come get you after his shift in a couple hours. You have his number right?"

She gulped back the first few things that popped into her head and did what her grandmother had taught her to so in this kind of situation. She dressed her crazy up a bit before she let it walk around. "I don't think I was being clear, Maxwell. If you don't come get me, then we're done. I need you. Don't choose an internship over me please."

"Frankie, what is going on with you? We talked about this. You were thrilled I got this opportunity, and you know exactly what it means for the rest of my career. It could be everything. You were going to support me. That's what you said."

"I'm happy to support you. I didn't realize it was going to be a one-way street. What happens when I have a bad day? You still don't know what's going on with my stuff, the things I came here for. A lot has changed, and you don't even ask. We might have found where the boyfriend who killed Danyia is. We could be on the verge of unraveling a conspiracy and finding a murderer. But that's not important, right?"

"I don't know if I'm supposed to be apologizing here or what. Because none of this should be a surprise to you. I've always been very upfront about my goals and what it would take to achieve them, and you've always told me you understood. Please don't give me an ultimatum. Don't ask me to choose right now." Maxwell's voice was desperate, and she knew why. He didn't want to have to tell her she'd end up on the wrong side of his choice.

"Where's your car?" she asked, accepting reality. "Give me the address where it's parked and leave the keys somewhere for me. I need to borrow it."

"I already told you Tao would come get you."

"He's working for two more hours and then he'll have a two-hour drive up here. I'm not going to sit here all that time and wallow in the fact that I . . ." she trailed off, not wanting to put a label on what was happening. Were they broken up? Were things over? She'd never understood people who left things unsaid. It always felt like a cop out, but she finally saw the advantages of being vague.

"I'll text you the info and leave the keys with the security guard for the parking garage." He assured some woman who was calling his name he was wrapping up this pesky inconvenient phone call. "I'll call you when I can."

"Whatever," she hissed back, but he was already gone from the line.

The crowd pouring in and out of the library was as constant as waves on the shore. That left her without an appropriate amount of time to scream bloody expletives at the top of her lungs. She settled instead for finding the nearest coffee shop and burying her troubles beneath three donuts. She wasn't starving; she was stalling. This was an attempt to talk herself out of the insane thing she was about to do. The sugar high, the rush of endorphins, would allow her better sense to start kicking in. But it never did.

She was hailing a cab a few minutes later, on her way to get Maxwell's car. She had a fire burning in her stomach, and it wasn't from the donuts. It was resolve. It was empowerment. And she was pretty sure it was also insane.

Chapter Seventeen

The GPS in her phone couldn't get a good enough signal to keep her on the right track. It was useless. Unlike most people her age however, her father had not let her depend on technology to navigate. When they had traveled he had insisted she'd unfold a good old-fashioned paper map and get her bearings. At the time, like most of the lessons he was teaching her, she never thought that would come in handy. But slowly over the years she found herself at an advantage over those around her who were far less prepared. She always had cash for an emergency. There was a granola bar in her bag at all times. She'd memorized phone numbers for everyone in her family in case she was ever without her handy speed dial on her cell phone. Time after time problems would arise, and without much thought she'd reach into the arsenal of wisdom her father had stocked her with and pull out something that made a difference.

Today, however, as Maxwell's car zoomed down the long, boring desert road she refused to acknowledge the connection between her skills and her father's teaching. Instead she focused on the signs she passed and the miles to go until she reached Coweherd Hill.

The radio was off, saving her from the vortex of sadness a sappy country song could pull her into. She hadn't exactly formed her plan yet, but she knew she had to do something. This trip wouldn't be in vain. If her family didn't want her back home, and if Maxwell couldn't make room for her, then she'd find her own purpose. She'd scale the damn sky and grab those stars and cram them in the bottle whether they liked it or not.

137

Her cell phone was ringing, and she wanted to be the kind of person who turned it off. If she was stronger, her willpower greater, she'd ignore it completely, but she couldn't lie to herself. She hoped maybe it was Maxwell coming to his senses. Or her father reconsidering his words now that he'd calmed down. But it wasn't either of them.

"It's not a good time right now, Tao," she said through pursed lips. They had to stay pursed because otherwise her chin would quiver, and she'd risk crying.

"Where are you?" he asked, talking over the loud engine of his mother's car. "I'm five minutes from the university."

"You're not supposed to be done at work yet," she argued as she looked down at the clock on the dashboard to make sure she wasn't going crazy. Had she bumped her head and lost two hours somehow?

"When my mom called I got the rest of my shift covered, and I hopped in the car," he explained. "I figured if you were upset I should hurry."

"You just got in the car?" she asked, wishing that kind of commitment was something you could sprinkle onto people who you wished had it.

"Wild horses," he said, and she could hear his smile. "Just tell me where you are, and I'll be there. We'll figure all this out. I'm sorry I gave you a hard time earlier. I have an opinion on how you should be treated, and I was worried you'd get less than you deserved. But that's not what I promised to do. I promised to have your back, no matter what."

"Maybe that is having my back," Frankie considered as she saw the road fork in front of her. "I'm not at the university. I borrowed Maxwell's car, and I'm headed to Cowherd."

"What?" Tao shouted. "Stop, Frankie. Pull the car over and stop what you're doing, so we can talk about this."

"I'm only fifteen minutes away, Tao. There's no point in stopping now. You aren't going to talk me out of this. I need it."

"You need what? If this is the guy who killed Danyia then he's a murderer, and you're going to go knock on his door? That's crazy. Just turn around and come back here. I told you the Tribal Police can transfer what we found to some federal contacts, I'm sure of it. You don't need to do this."

"I've based the last four years of my life on this. Not this case, not Danyia, but on the idea that I will be a good journalist. Everything else is falling apart. Maybe I picked the wrong guy. Maybe I overestimated my parents' patience and love. I need to know this part of my plan still makes sense. I can't come out of this completely empty-handed."

"You're not. You can come out of this with me. I know I'm not the guy you've been dreaming about for the last few years. But you deserve to have someone who will show up. And I'll show up. Just give me the chance. Pull over and wait for me. We can do this together." Tao was speaking with such rushed urgency she felt sorry for putting him through this.

"Tao, I'm not sure how I would have gotten through this trip without you," she started but when she looked at her screen she could see the call had dropped. *No service.*

She took the fork in the road that went left and considered pulling over. Would he remember the address they'd found yesterday? Would he be able to find her? If she turned the car around she could drive back to an area with better service, and make a plan with him. But the car kept driving, fueled by her frustration with herself.

She glanced at the map and the red line she'd drawn on it. She was getting closer, and her next turn off was only a couple miles ahead of her. Best case, Tao was an hour and ten minutes behind her. She could be at the address in a few minutes. Maybe she'd just drive by.

Pulling past the sign that declared this a town of 304 residents, Frankie was struck by the world she'd entered and how much it reminded her of another place she'd been. When she was fourteen years old she and her father had volunteered to do clean up on the gulf coast after a devastating hurricane. He'd brought her to one of the poorest areas that had been hit, and to call it a humbling experience would be an understatement. That trip had been her father's way of teaching her the subtle difference between poverty and extreme poverty. That was something she hadn't realized still existed in this country. He'd also shown her that not all wealthy people are fortunate, just like not all poor people are unfortunate. You can be happy and grateful no matter how little you have.

Before that trip her dad had always been just her dad. Being on the cleaning crew the first time, she watched him do things that inspired her in an incredible way. For a tall man, he could crouch himself down to the lowest level, meeting the eyes of an elderly woman in a wheelchair or holding the hand of a scared toddler. He'd rolled up his sleeves and had worked like dog, sweat pouring from his head and blood trailing down his arms from a cut on his hand from a piece of twisted metal that had pinned a dog, trapping it for two days. Michael Cooper, the lawyer, the man who knew a good bottle of wine from a bad one, put his back into helping people who were hurting on the inside as much as they were on the outside. From that moment on Frankie knew she was very lucky to be the child of a good man.

This place reminded her where they'd been. It hadn't been hit by a hurricane, but it might as well have been for the state the houses were in. Their roofs were puzzle pieces of rusted sheet metal latched together. The asphalt road ended abruptly, and she drove across the barren orange dirt, kicking up dust in her wake.

She hadn't noticed the asphalt was about to end. It just stopped all at once before she could do anything about it. She blinked away the tears. Could the man who had spent her whole life saying he was proud of her, that she was just like him, really give up on her? Had that road finally end too?

Tartin Lane came up on her left, and she drew in a deep breath. The property in question would be a quarter mile up on the left. If she was going to go back and call Tao, it was now or never. She convinced herself to drive down the road and take a quick look at the house. Then she could decide from there.

She gripped the steering wheel to keep the tremble in her hands at bay. There was only one house on the road, and it could have been easily missed since it was covered with tall, overgrown grassy shrubs. Was it intentionally camouflaged to hide a killer? She slowed down to get a good look at the property, but there wasn't much to see. The roof, like the others she'd seen, was a patchwork of rusty metal. The chimney was in disrepair, half of it toppled over. There were a few broken-down cars parked in a carport, no longer with a canopy over it. Any type of path leading to the house had long since been hidden by gnarled and twisted branches of bushes. This place looked like the hollowed-out remnants of a bad dream.

Double-checking, not wanting to look away, she craned her neck as she tried for one last look. Considering there were no other houses on the street she assumed, incorrectly of course, that the other side of the road would be fairly clear. She heard the smashing of glass as a metal rod broke through the passenger window, sending shattered pieces of thick glass onto the seat like falling snow. Another rod came through the metal of the door and poked a few inches past the leather of the interior. The car had been pierced. A trap, she wondered? Did this murderer treat his prey like flies, snaring them in a web before attacking?

"No," she yelled, begging for time to rewind just a few seconds so this had not just happened. Fear of being stuck outweighed the reality of damaging Maxwell's car.

Staring at the two pieces of metal she tried to figure out what the hell it was and what it was doing there. When she realized it didn't really matter she backed the car up quickly, but the metal had come in at such an angle it couldn't seem to get itself back out, no matter how she gunned the gas. She'd have to get out of the car and try to pull it out.

"You all right?" a man asked as he tapped on her window, and she screamed without thinking how silly she might sound. "Sorry to scare you," he said, tossing his hands up disarmingly. She rolled her window down an inch and tried to form a sentence, but his face registered in her brain, working like a plug stopping the words. This was Denver. He was older, his hair had thinned considerably, and his eyes were sunken a little farther, but this was him. She was right. He was alive. His uncle had hidden him here. And suddenly none of that mattered because he wasn't a story to break now, he was a murderer who was standing just a few inches from her, and she was trapped.

"Are you hurt?" he asked, trying to read her face.

"No," she choked out. "I'm so dumb I didn't see this giant piece of metal. I'm good. I'm just going to go."

"It looks like you won't get very far unless we get that out of your car first. Someone dumped it here the other day. I don't even know what it is. I just haven't had time to move it yet." The man moved in front of her car and began inspecting the metal that was trapping her. "Oh damn, it's attached to a bunch of old railroad ties. I don't have anything here that can move that. I'll give Sammy a call and have him come down with his tractor. The way the metal went in he'll have to pull all this junk out, and the metal should come with it."

"I have to go," Frankie said as though that decree would give her more options than were actually available.

"This isn't exactly a through street. We don't get a lot of traffic, obviously, so can I ask what you're doing here?" It didn't make sense to Frankie. This man had kind, soft blue eyes and the type of smile that could disarm you of any worry. Nothing about him screamed cold-blooded killer. But it didn't stop the hair on the back of her neck from standing at attention.

"I'm lost," she lied. "I was leaving the university and coming up to visit my boyfriend and my GPS stopped working."

"That's the problem these days, no one knows what to do without those damn phones. Why don't you come inside, and I'll get Sammy here."

"Why would I go inside?" she asked, her eyes wide with fear.

"It's a hundred six degrees outside, and you have," he leaned in the smashed passenger window and looked at her dashboard, "about a quarter tank of gas and there isn't a station close to here, so I wouldn't suggest you sit out here running your air conditioner, nor would I suggest you sit out here and not run your air conditioner. Unless you like to fry eggs on your forehead."

"I'm fine. I'll be fine; thanks anyway." She held her phone up as high as she could in the car trying to will it to have service suddenly.

"I'm sorry," he said, lowering his body so that he was more at her level. "You're lost, and you just damaged your car, and I'm some stranger. I'll see if Mary is over at the rec center. You can wait there. It was stupid to think you'd be comfortable in my house. I'll be right back."

It seems easy to assume that you know how you'll react when your life is in danger but your mind doesn't account for the gray area. Am I in danger? Am I reading this wrong? If Frankie had been asked about this scenario yesterday, she'd have said she'd be running right now. The car door would've flown open, and she would've been screaming her head off while she weaved her way to something that looked like civilization and help. But she was frozen. And before she could talk herself into any kind of action Denver was back at her window. "Miss Mary will be here in a couple minutes. My name is Doug, by the way. I'm sorry again for rattling you. You're not from around here are you?"

"No sir," she replied, nervously fiddling with her cell phone. "I'm from back east."

"Are you coming to school out here?" he asked, and though the question seemed innocuous and the situation seemed tense, Frankie couldn't help but cough out a laugh.

"That's the million dollar question. I'm not really sure yet." Her eyes danced between the man and the rearview mirror, trying to keep an eye on her surroundings.

"I don't envy you. I wouldn't want to be a kid your age these days. The whole world is going off the rails." Denver/Doug chuckled.

"I'm sure you had your own share of troubles," she replied confidently as she watched for the slightest twitch in his face. But there was nothing.

"Suppose every generation does. Oh look, here's Miss Mary."

"Oh you poor thing," the woman sang as she came around to Frankie's car door and opened it. "Doug will get your car out of this mess and cleaned up, and you can stay over at the rec center with me while he does." Miss Mary looked like she wasn't much older than Frankie. Her long blond hair danced to the bottom of her back, and besides the crooked teeth she flashed, she was stunningly perfect.

"Thank you," Frankie said genuinely, as though this girl had just pulled her from, the clutches of a grizzly bear. "And you as well," she said to Denver/Doug as an afterthought as they moved across the street.

The rec center was no more than an old tiny storefront that had been cleared out and filled with books and board games. A few wobbly fold-out tables and some mismatched chairs filled the middle of the room.

"It's not much," Mary admitted, looking embarrassed. "But we work hard to keep the air conditioner running so it's a cool place for the kids to come. They are the first to remind me though; it's cool only in temperature. It's not cool in any other way."

Frankie laughed and took the bottle of water Mary was offering. It wasn't cold, but she was dying of thirst.

"I'm sorry that junk got caught up in your car. People from other towns treat this place like it's a dump, and they drop junk on the side of the roads. What brings you here anyway? I can't remember the last time we had a stranger roll in to Cowherd." Frankie had thought Mary to be meek and welcoming, but a glint in her eye just flashed the truth. Mary was trying to pin down what Frankie's deal was and whether or not she was a threat.

"I got lost. The stupid GPS lost the signal, and I am just useless with a map." Frankie took a long draw of the bottle of water, trying to lead the conversation back to Mary.

"Don't you worry, we'll get you all squared away and make sure you have good directions out of here. That's what you want, right?" Mary raised an eyebrow at her.

"Of course. I just want to be on my way," Frankie assured her.

"You don't have any business here?" Mary pressed, taking a few steps closer to Frankie.

"What business would I have?" Frankie asked in her favorite defense of answering a question with a question.

"None," Mary answered, waving off the idea. "Of course you wouldn't have any. Doug will get you all squared away."

"He seems nice," Frankie said as she put the water bottle down and began browsing the tattered books on the shelf. "Have you known him long?"

"You could say that," Mary said, her tone changing slightly, just enough for Frankie to notice it. "He's my father."

"Really?" Frankie asked, not spinning around to look at Mary to check for similar features. "I wouldn't have guessed that because he called you Miss Mary. But to be honest, I pictured an old lady when he said that."

Mary laughed though Frankie could tell it was forced. "I run the daycare here so everyone just got in the habit of calling me Miss Mary. I hate to leave you here, but I need to run a couple of quick errands. Help yourself to more water from the fridge and any book that interests you." Mary leaned over one of the tables and grabbed a huge set of keys that would make a janitor jealous.

Before Frankie could thank her for the hospitality, Mary was gone. Something was wrong here. The most important lesson her father ever taught her was to trust her gut feelings. Again she considered running, but talked herself out of it. The heat would kill her. Checking her cell phone once more she sighed. How did people live here without cell service?

After hunting around for a landline for ten minutes she finally gave up. Grabbing a book from the shelf, she swigged back the rest of her water and tried to keep herself calm. But more time continued to tick by, and Mary still wasn't back. No one had come to tell her the car was free from the scrap metal snare. Twenty minutes turned into an hour, and hospitality started to feel a lot more like imprisonment.

She stuck her head into the back room again and started considering what her exit strategy would be if this went bad. She saw a stack of white bread slices and a jar of peanut butter in the corner of the room. Next to it was the gleaming metal of a small kitchen knife. It wasn't much, but at least she could conceal it, and if jabbed in someone's eye it could end up saving her life.

Walking with purpose and swift feet, she crossed the small back room toward the knife. When the front door clattered as though it had been kicked in, she froze. There was only a tiny window at the back of the room, too small for her to squeeze her body through. If someone meant her harm right now they had the upper hand. She was trapped.

Chapter Eighteen

"Where is she?" Tao's voice, deeper than usual, boomed through the tiny rec center. "You have three seconds to tell me."

"Kid, calm down," she heard Doug plead as another loud bang shook the floor. "I told you I sent her in here to be with my daughter while I waited for the tractor."

"Tao," Frankie whispered, trying to build her voice back up through the suffocating fear.

At the sight of her, Tao's face went from tight and fierce to relieved. He had the man in a headlock so tight his face was an unnatural shade of red. "Go to my car," Tao ordered her and she moved fast, tripping on her own feet as she went.

When her hand hit the cool brass knob on the door someone else spun it first and shoved their weight into it, sending her backward. Crashing into Tao, she knew her portal to freedom had just evaporated in front of her.

Mary slammed the door behind her and locked it as she raised her hand up toward them. She held a small gun with the steadiness of a statue. "Let him go," she demanded, pointing the gun straight at Tao.

"Not until Frankie gets outside," he demanded. "Let her by you, and when I see she's at the car I'll let him go."

Mary shook her head as though his words meant nothing. Rather than arguing back her own terms, she read the situation and shifted her aim, lining the gun up with Frankie's head.

Though this was the first time Frankie had ever had a weapon pointed at her, she did not let Mary's subtle

149

brilliance get lost in her fear. Tao had pointed out what was important to him, and Mary used that to her advantage.

"Let him go," Mary said again, this time enunciating every syllable and tightening her grip on the gun. Tao had no choice; he loosened his grip on the man and shoved him forward. Then, just as quickly, he grabbed Frankie and tucked her behind him.

"What the hell is going on here?" Doug asked as he rubbed at his neck where Tao had nearly squeezed the life out of him.

"Nothing," Frankie insisted, raising her hands up disarmingly. "We are just in the wrong place at the wrong time, and there has clearly been some kind of miscommunication. Just let us go, and we'll send a tow truck for the car later."

"Bull," Mary shouted. "No one takes a wrong turn and ends up here. Now who are you, and why were you trying to hurt Doug?"

"I pulled up and saw the car with the smashed window," Tao explained. "I thought he'd done something to Frankie."

"Why would he do something to her?" Mary asked, raising an eyebrow, challenging them to try to convince her of something.

Frankie considered holding firm to her commitment to play dumb. But she could probably give an award winning performance and still Mary would have that gun pointed at them. "His name isn't really Doug," she stuttered. "His name is Denver Stills; isn't that right?" She turned toward the man and pressed him with her eyes, but he didn't speak. Mary did.

"I know that," she growled. "The question is how do you know that, and why do you care?"

"He killed a girl seventeen years ago, and he's been hiding out here ever since," Tao said, jumping in before Frankie could. If this girl was crazy or something he clearly wanted to be the bearer of bad news and shield Frankie.

"You need to tell them," she directed, staring at Denver/Doug expectantly. "You've suffered enough years for this; you don't need to make it worse."

"No," Denver/Doug dismissed. "Just let them go on their way, Mary. Put the gun down and let them go. You'll make it all worse."

"Dad, they'll have the police here in no time, and you'll be gone. You've been punished enough. We can't let them go." Mary's eyes were filling fast with tears. Frankie could usually sort out scenarios quickly, but this one did not make any sense. Mary was too old to be his daughter. He'd have moved here seventeen years ago when he didn't have any kids, and she was at least in her twenties.

"Mary, please," he pleaded. "You're not going to fix this for me. I know you feel like you owe me so much because I took you in after your mom died, but that's not the case. You aren't my keeper. Maybe it's time I face this."

"Fine, but face it with the truth." Mary took a step toward him and slapped her hand to the table. You aren't disposable. Don't trade your life to protect a secret. Tell them."

"It sounds like there is more to the story than we know," Tao said slowly. "So why don't you put down the gun, and we can sit down and talk about it."

"I'm not putting this down until my father agrees to tell the truth." She turned to Denver/Doug. "If you want this to end then you give me that." Mary kept her arm raised and steady as they all stared at the gun she was gripping tightly.

"Put it down, Mary. I'll give you what you want." He hung his head and pulled out one of the old schoolhouse chairs. "You first," he instructed. "I'm not sitting here talking while you're waving a gun around."

Mary's eyes darted between Frankie and Tao, looking like she was trying to size them up. She gestured for the two of them to sit down but both of them shook their heads no.

"You're Tewapia?" he asked Tao, who replied with just a grunt and a nod. "So you must know Danyia's family. You've heard the stories?"

"The only thing I've ever heard was she was dating you, you killed her, and then you died in a car accident before they could arrest you. Not many people on the reservation bought that story, but they didn't have many options."

"No," he agreed, "people on the reservation don't have many options. I grew up on the line that separated the land. I saw how tortured many of the Tewapia were. I also saw how my family and friends treated them. When I was nine my folks moved to California to join some commune, and my uncle refused to let them take me. He was stern, but he cared about me. He worked as a police officer and did his job honorably."

"Including helping you fake your death so you could get away with murder?" Frankie asked as she folded her arms across her chest.

"That's the problem with your generation. You accept the easiest version of every story because your attention span isn't long enough to stick around to find out more. There are many different sides to the same story."

"Yeah," Mary agreed. "That's why he had to leave and hide out here."

Frankie rolled her eyes, wondering how many years it took a guy like Denver to completely turn into Doug. Did it happen all at once, or had he slowly become this new person? And how long did it take to get Mary to blindly follow him?

"I met Danyia when we were both fourteen. I had never seen any girl as beautiful. She had come off the reservation to buy some seeds for her mother's garden from the store by my house. Some guys hassled her, and I offered to walk her home. From that moment on we were connected to each other in a way I've never been able to explain." Frankie looked over at Tao and thought of that first night on the rocks when she felt like a piece of her fused to him.

"We'd sneak off together. Danyia was so full of life and energy, but sometimes she was also painfully sad. It was hard to watch because I didn't know how to cheer her up. The more time we spent together the better I thought I understood it. Her father was a drunk and beat on her and her mother. He died when we were sixteen after falling from some scaffolding. I thought that would help her shake some of the darkness, but it only made it worse."

Tao was staring at him intensely, not wanting to miss a single twitch of the eye or pulse of the vein in his forehead—his own version of a lie detector test.

"Your uncle didn't mind you dating her?" Frankie asked, remembering Lila's description of the miserable, racist old man.

"He forbade it, actually, when he found out." He laughed and tipped his head back. "You two might not be old enough to have experienced this yet, but when someone forbids you to do something it's like gasoline on a fire. It fueled us even more. We snuck around, and as time went by we fell very deeply in love. But something snapped in Danyia one day. She had this kind of mental breakdown when we were walking back to her place through the woods. I still don't know, even to this day, what set her off."

"What do you mean, a mental breakdown?" Frankie pushed, not giving this man's story an ounce of credibility yet.

"She started hearing voices I think. There were hallucinations involved, I remember. I had to pick her up and carry her the rest of the way back to her house. I practically kicked in her door and scared the life out of her mother. I have never seen anyone go through something like that before. I was seventeen, I think."

He stopped speaking abruptly and ran his hand over his mouth a few times, trying to gather himself.

"What was she diagnosed with?" Frankie asked, hoping to catch him in a lie.

"Nothing," he explained, throwing his hands up in exasperation. "That day they called the elders and the medicine man and tried to calm her. There was a special tea and some ceremonies, and eventually she fell asleep. I begged them to take her to the hospital. But they refused. They just kept saying her spirit had shifted, and she needed to be rebalanced. The treatment was just nonsense."

Tao's body language shifted rigidly as he took exception to what was being said. "The Tewapia people inhabited this land for thousands of years before it was stolen. In those years we managed to be healthy and survive even here in the desert. Our traditions in medicine are not nonsense."

"You're right," Denver agreed, nodding vigorously. "I just think in Danyia's case there could have been a more modern intervention that could have helped her. But they all refused."

Tao let out an annoyed chuckle. "It isn't that people on the reservation don't want modern intervention for their medical problems. It's that it can't be done hand in hand with what they practice and believe. Tewapia treatments are dismissed as voodoo and nonsense. The two have to be exclusive of each other. You can't get mainstream medical treatment without walking away from your own beliefs."

"We're getting off topic," Mary warned as she banged the butt of the gun against the table.

"Danyia got better for a little while," Denver continued. "She was happy again, and things started to get back on track. I got an apartment of my own, and she started coming over more and more. I ignored my uncle's attempts to keep us apart, and we made it work. We were happy. Until she started to sink again. She was manic and terrified. I took her to the hospital, and they admitted her to the psych ward. Within thirty minutes her family was having her discharged into their care. They claimed it went against their beliefs to have her treated there. I never saw her alive again after she walked out those hospital doors. Two days later I came home to find her lying in a pool of her own blood that had spilled from her slit wrists. I was devastated." Denver stood and turned his back on them all. Frankie couldn't tell if he was crying and, worse than that, she couldn't read his face to see if he was telling the truth.

"No," Tao whispered and then changed quickly into his second language as he rattled through what she thought sounded like prayers or chants.

"You know what she wrote in the letter she left me, don't you?" Denver asked, sucking in his lower lip and gnawing on it nervously.

"What?" Frankie asked, turning her face up toward Tao's.

"She'd have asked him to make sure her family never knew she killed herself. In the Tewapia culture it is believed that a person who ends his or her own life is banished to an existence worse than anything you can imagine. More than that, every generation of her bloodline before her who has passed away would be taken from their restful peace and thrown into turmoil. I can't think of a single thing in your culture to compare it to." Tao looked out the window and chanted a few more words before glancing toward Denver. Frankie could tell that if she didn't completely believe the man yet, Tao did.

"Where's the letter?" Frankie asked, sending a message to her friend that he might be jumping the gun with his absolution of Denver.

"I still have it. It's at my house. I'll be happy to show it to you. In it she asked me to do specific things to cleanse her body and her spirit. Things I'd assume only a Tewapia person would know."

"And where is her body? That's what her mother wants. That's the peace she's looking for." Frankie hadn't forgotten the presence of a gun, but she also remembered the look on Chari's face when she talked about not having her daughter's body. That emboldened her to keep pressing on for more information.

"She didn't want her family to know what she'd done. I believe she'd still like to protect them from the truth. That's why I did what she asked. I cleaned up the scene, performed a few rituals the best I could and buried her in the desert. I knew it might blow back on me, and I might get thrown in jail. That was something I was willing to face to protect her secret, but my uncle had other ideas. I never told him what happened, he insisted I not tell him anything about it. I'm guessing he just figured I killed her. He promised that if it came down to it, he'd protect me."

"Where did you bury her?" Frankie pressed, ignoring his attempt at changing the subject.

"Frankie," Tao said softly. "You don't understand what the truth would do to Chari. There is no real way for me to explain it, but the woman you saw the other day in that trailer, she wouldn't survive this."

Mary let out an arrogant huff. "Now you see why I didn't want you to run out of here declaring you found a murderer. He's spent almost two decades in this barren rundown place all to protect Danyia and her family. That's all the punishment he needs."

"There isn't much to corroborate what you're saying though, is there?" Frankie countered. "Maybe forensically, with the note and her writing samples, they'll be able to prove it through."

"There isn't going to be a trial or forensics," Tao asserted. "There isn't going to be anything. I'll look at the note and see if it's genuinely reflecting Tewapia beliefs and rituals after death. If this is what Danyia wanted, we should leave things as they are."

"Tao, this man is technically a fugitive since there were warrants out for his arrest. The case needs to be brought to trial, and they need to vet out what he's said. All he's done is make a statement. We have no reason to believe it's the truth." Frankie squeezed Tao's arm to try to bring him back to her side of the argument, but the look in his eye spoke volumes.

"I believe him," Tao announced, and he stared down at Frankie hoping she'd agree.

"We need to have the police come. They'll take his statement, and he can lead them to the remains. Then they'll investigate and decide if charges should be pressed." Frankie laid out the only logical solution. "We aren't judge and jury here."

"You are not calling the police," Mary asserted, raising the gun and pointing it at Frankie again.

"Mary, put it down." Denver's voice was firm, and he pointed a stern finger at her. "If you call the police I won't tell them what I just told you. It's been almost two decades of keeping this secret for her sake, and I'm not going to betray that now. They can toss me in jail and try me for murder, but I won't divulge what she asked me not to."

"That's moronic," Frankie choked out. "You're going to spend the rest of your life in jail for a crime you didn't commit and still not tell them where the body is? That's your choice. It changes nothing for me."

"We need a minute," Tao announced as he grabbed Frankie's arm and pulled her toward the door. Mary blocked it with her body but acquiesced when Denver gestured for her to let them go.

The wall of heat slammed Frankie in the face when they stepped out the door into the hot desert sun.

"There is no point in dragging all this up. You'll have to trust that I know better than you about the Tewapia people. This will not help Chari; it will hurt her. Destroy her."

"And that's sad," Frankie admitted. "But we just found a man who's been hiding for seventeen years. We have a responsibility to tell this story."

"I get it now, this is a story to you, something you can put your name on. A badge for the sash you plan to wear around college. These are *people,* Frankie, and yes they have different beliefs than you, but those beliefs are sacred to them. To me. If you think that telling this story is worth destroying Danyia's family, then you are nothing like I thought you were."

"You don't get to pick and choose what stories you tell when you're a journalist. You just report." She thought she'd go toe to toe with him on this, but the boom in his voice let her know she was not likely to keep up.

"You are not a reporter, you're a kid. Have some compassion for what these people have been through and help find a way to make this work for everyone without putting yourself in that equation. You are the cleverest person I've ever met, and if you really looked at this problem I know you can find a solution. You just have to put what you want, what you think is so important,

159

aside." Tao's anger lessoned like a deflating balloon the more he spoke.

"What are you asking me?" Frankie questioned, pushing her hair off her sweaty forehead.

"He didn't kill her. I believe that. I can't explain exactly why but something is telling me he didn't. So I don't believe he deserves to go to jail for the rest of his life. But I also heard him say he would do that and not betray Danyia if we call the cops. Her mother wants her body so she can have peace. There has to be a way to navigate this. Right?" Tao wasn't shouting demands anymore, he was begging. He wanted so badly to keep people from hurting.

Frankie let her brain begin working even though it was bogged down by the heat and wasn't convinced this was a good idea. "The decomposition of a body is accelerated in heat. Danyia wasn't embalmed, I'm assuming, and she was likely buried right in the dirt with noting to protect her from the elements. If that's the case, her remains would be just skeletal now. It would be highly unlikely to determine she slit her wrist, causing her death. I don't think returning the body to Chari will betray Danyia's secret anymore." Frankie worked through the other issues in her head the way she did with any problem. "But alerting the police to the location of the body without divulging how we got the information will be a problem."

She tapped her foot the way she always did when she was trying to get her brain working in overdrive. "Thank you," Tao hummed as he pulled her into his arms, their overheated bodies sticking together.

"I haven't figured it out yet," she warned.

"But you will." Tao smiled. She tipped her head back and stared into his eyes. He was here. He showed up when she needed someone, and more than that, he kept trying to guide her away from the path consumed by her own selfish drive.

"You sounded really scared when you didn't know where I was. It looked like you were about to pop Denver's head off his shoulders."

Tao chuckled. "I would have if I hadn't found you. If he'd have hurt you I would have hurt him worse."

"I'm really glad I met you. I think I needed to be reminded what it's like to have someone who shows up and sticks around when it's important."

His hand came up toward her face and his thumb brushed over her chin, tilting it up slightly. "I want to ki—" he started, but her lips rose up toward his and dammed the words in his mouth.

Maybe it was the tension that had built between them or the high stakes this situation had created, but they kissed as though it would recharge life in them. Like their battery lights had flashed dangerously low, and this would be all they needed. Her hands looped up around his neck and his around her waist, pulling her in tight to his body. If not for the tap on the window that pulled them back to reality, it might have gone on forever.

When they broke apart an awkward laugh was all each could manage as they tried to wrestle out the right words.

"Is it bad that I want a thousand more of those, but I'm not sure you'll even be around long enough to give them to me?" Tao cleared his throat, which was filling up with embarrassing vulnerability.

"It's not bad at all."

161

Chapter Nineteen

"What did you do?" Jules asked as she came shooting like a cannonball through his office door.

Michael had barely found a way to stop his hands from shaking let alone ready himself for this argument. "Jules, honey, can we talk about this tonight?" he pleaded, running his hands though his hair, the stress crushing him.

"No," she replied sternly. "We will talk about this now. If you have a meeting cancel it. You just told our daughter not to come home. That can't wait."

"You had to hear the conversation," Michael defended. "She has this warped sense of how the world works. I had to make a point."

"And that's the one you went with? Because it's not at all what we've agreed to over the years. We've always said our parenting philosophy was built on the premise that she'd always have a soft place to fall when she needed it. The odds that she'll make this situation work with Maxwell are pretty damn slim. Do you know what happens when that falls apart and she doesn't feel like she can come back here? She moves on to the next mistake, a bigger one."

"She lied to us," Michael countered. "I'm not talking small, either. She applied to a school and was planning her life without giving us so much as a second thought."

"And that hurts like hell," Jules admitted. "But I don't care if she robbed a bank, we are her parents. She will never screw up so much she can't come to us when she needs to. You made this unilateral decision, and you need to fix it."

"I think some tough love is in order." Michael leaned back in his chair and crossed his arms over his chest. A move made to show his unwavering opinion on the matter but also functional, because if his wife got mad enough she might just reach into his chest and rip his heart out with her bare hands.

But like the last twenty years of his life, Jules did not disappoint. The woman could argue a point with the best of them, and that was saying something considering Michael was a lawyer. "My heart is broken too," she sighed as she rounded his desk and rubbed the stress from his shoulder. "I'm devastated that we're losing our little girl. But take it from someone who knows. I went through this myself, and she's not doing it on purpose. The only thing that got me through those years was my mother continuing to let me know, no matter what, her door was open. This won't be the last time Frankie hurts us, but it could certainly be the last time she turns to us for help if we don't handle it correctly."

"We did so many things right," Michael choked out as he dropped his face into his palms. "She's my baby, and I don't even recognize her right now. Why does she want to be so far away?"

"Because Maxwell is there," Jules explained, squeezing his shoulder tighter. "She has tunnel vision right now. We had to know this was coming. She's been all about this boy for years. We did the right thing by making her wait until she was older to be with him, but we also made him the forbidden fruit. He's a good kid, but at some point Frankie is going to realize the dream she's built up in her mind isn't real. No one, no matter how good he is, can live up to that fantasy. Our job isn't to protect her from that, it's to make sure she knows where to turn."

"I've always been the most important guy in her life. I knew that couldn't last forever, but I'm not ready." Michael leaned his head over to his wife and rested it on her shoulder. "How do people do this?"

"I have no idea," Jules admitted somberly. "Maybe Ian will stay with us forever. He tells me all the time he wants to live with Mommy and Daddy his whole life."

Michael looked at the photograph of his family on his desk. The fantastic four they called themselves, and now one of them was breaking away. "Let's make him sign a contract now. Something ironclad." Michael spun his desk chair and pulled Jules into his lap, holding her tight as though she were a lifesaver and somehow buoy him to safety.

"Can I make her sweat it out for a few days at least?" Michael asked, batting his lashes at his wife.

"Yes," Jules agreed. "She deserves to sweat a little for putting us through this hell. You know what we did wrong all these years, right?"

Michael's brows furrowed as though Jules had been holding some priceless knowledge that could have saved them all of this pain.

"We made her too self-sufficient. She worked and earned money from the moment she was old enough. We taught her how to travel. We showed her how to take care of herself. The last eighteen years we've worked to make her ready for the world. We made her brave and confident. What we should have done is made her completely helpless, penniless, and afraid of everything."

"Would that have worked?" Michael asked, a flash of hope in his eyes that maybe it wasn't too late to reverse everything they'd done.

"No," she whispered into her husband's hair. "She still would have left, she just would have been less prepared and more likely to get hurt. We did the right thing. It's just time to start dealing with the fact that she's going to start putting all these lessons and pep talks into play."

"I miss her," Michael grunted as a rogue tear traced its way down his cheek. "When all this other crap is over, and we sort it out, I'm still going to miss her."

"Me too," Jules cried, letting her emotions untether and fly free. She buried her face in Michael's neck, and they sat in each other's arms, mourning the moments that couldn't be recaptured.

"Other parents must have survived this," Michael said. "We will too."

"Let's go pick Ian up from summer camp early and go to a movie like we used to do with Frankie," Jules suggested.

"That sounds good," Michael agreed. "But let's just sit here one more minute. I'm not ready yet."

Chapter Twenty

"This sounds like it could work," Tao said, trying to spread his optimism around the room.

"I'm not sure," Frankie countered. "Calling in an anonymous tip, leading authorities to the body seems risky. There is so much technology now. If they link it back to you, Denver, then you won't be safe here."

Denver shook his head. "I don't intend to be here. When Mary's mom died ten years ago, she had nowhere to go. I was alone, just falling apart really. We both needed something in our lives, and it worked out. But I told her the truth right away. I didn't think it was fair to take her in without her knowing all the things that could happen. She's always known the day might come when we'd move on. I'm actually shocked it took this long. But if it were this easy for you to find me, then once they find Danyia's remains, others might take an interest and do the same. Mary and I will pack up tonight, be out of here in the morning, and somewhere along the way I'll call it in. Then we'll be gone." Denver looked over at Mary as if to make sure she didn't have any objections.

"I'm sick of this crappy little town anyway." She smirked. "We can start over somewhere new."

"Once they recover her remains Chari will be able to bury her properly and perform all the rituals she wants to?" Frankie asked Tao who nodded, the corners of his mouth turning up in a big smile. "And Denver will be gone, off the radar, and he can go on with his life. So everyone gets what they need." Frankie didn't say *everyone but me*. She didn't need to. Tao could see that this, while a victory, would fall short of Frankie's expectations of this trip and herself. Something that had become a pattern for her since coming out to Arizona.

Denver, assuming this was another perk, chimed in. "And the two of you will have nothing to do with this. It'll be like this never happened. You can go back to your own lives."

Tao watched Frankie intentionally keep her face from falling into a sad grimace. "Thank goodness," she agreed.

"Now, I'm having your car towed back to a shop in the university area," Denver said as though everything were settled now. "You should be all set then."

"Thank you," Tao said, standing up and shaking his hand. "I appreciate what you did for Danyia and her family. I know it must not have been easy. You gave up a lot to protect what her family thought of her and to try to give them peace."

"When I look back on the time I had with her I still can't believe how deeply I loved her. It feels like a dream. She was on my mind all the time, and I felt lucky to have even a minute of her attention. I'm surprised she cared about me. She was my first love, and I don't think this happens often, but she was also my best love. The true love of my life." Denver looked out the window nostalgically and got lost in his memories.

Frankie's thoughts went to Maxwell. He was her first love. She felt lucky to get his attention and was surprised he cared so much for her. Was he the best love of her life? Was she giving up on them too easily? She should have known Tao's eyes would be on her, and she should have guessed he'd be insightful enough to realize what she was thinking.

"Ready?" he asked her, pulling open the door and gesturing for her to go first. They settled in silence into his car and headed back toward civilization.

"Listen," he started, turning the radio down so there would be no distractions. "That kiss, I don't want to throw your whole world into craziness right now. I get you're going through something, and you are still trying to figure it out. I didn't plan to make any of that harder for you."

"You wish we didn't kiss?" she asked, holding her breath and bracing for the answer.

"You could drag me over burning coals while you stabbed me with toothpicks, and I wouldn't let you take that kiss back," he laughed. "I'm not saying I regret it. Just don't feel like you owe me anything right now. I care about you, and I hope that first kiss doesn't turn out to be our last, but I can see you still have to figure things out with Maxwell." Tao looked straight ahead, not even glancing at her as he spoke.

"I can't tell you how much that means to me," she emphasized, touching his arm gently. "I wouldn't let you take that kiss back either, but I'm also not sure exactly what it means. I need to sort this out."

As they drove farther away from the quiet dirt road, Tao's phone rose from the dead and began chirping. "My mom," Tao said, turning the screen toward her. "Can you text her and let her know we're still in the university area. I'll wait until the car gets towed and you have time to tell Maxwell about it, then we can head back."

She started typing the message back but stopped when her own phone started to ring. "It's Maxwell," she apologized as she put it up to her ear and wished she had room to get out of earshot. Impossible in a car.

"Hey Maxwell, I have something to tell you about your car." She gulped back her nerves and forged ahead. "I was just driving, kind of clearing my head and I got lost on some back road. I hit a piece of metal, and it came through the passenger window and door."

"Are you all right?" Maxwell asked, and she was so relieved this was his first question. That had to mean something.

"I'm fine. Tao came up to get me, and I'm having the car towed to a shop close to you. I can cover all the expenses; it was totally my fault."

"Who cares," Maxwell cut in. "I'm just glad you weren't hurt. I'm so sorry about earlier. I was acting like a jerk. You came all the way out here, you listened to everything I had to say about this internship, and I never even asked you about how things were going for you. This is hard, but we can find a way to get through it. I managed to get a couple hours off for dinner tonight. Will you stay and come eat with me? I know we can work this out if we just have some time to talk."

"I, um . . . tonight?" she asked, stalling as she turned her head toward the window as if that might get her more privacy. "I guess I could do that. It's just that Tao is my ride back to his house."

"I'll get you a ride back. Trust me, that's no big deal. The only thing that matters to me right now is making this right with you. Please, give me another chance to do that." Maxwell had his old determined spark back in his voice and Frankie had missed that.

"Of course," she proclaimed, not wanting him to think she had any reservations about it. It wasn't likely he'd assume she'd just kissed someone else, but she wasn't taking any chances. "I'll be there. Text me when you're ready. I'm sorry again about the car."

"No big deal. Oh, tell Tao thanks for helping you out. He's a good guy for watching out for my girl."

"I'll tell him," Frankie assured him, saying goodbye and hanging up the phone.

"He wants to do dinner tonight. He actually took time off so we could talk. He said he was sorry." Frankie adjusted the vents on the air conditioner so they were blasting right at her hot cheeks.

"Good," Tao said, nodding his head as though he was trying to convince himself.

"He said, um . . . to tell you—" Frankie started, but Tao waved her off.

"Please don't," Tao cut in, not elaborating on why he wanted her to stop talking. She assumed he didn't want to be thanked by her boyfriend for being a good *pal* in her time of need.

"If you want to drop me off at the library I think he'll meet me there. Then he said he'll get me a ride back to your house later tonight." Frankie couldn't look at Tao as she spoke. He'd been so good to her, and after that kiss maybe he thought she was done with Maxwell. She had to admit, in the middle of that kiss, she probably forgot who Maxwell even was. But she wasn't ready to walk away from him yet.

"Are you going to tell him?" Tao asked, finally looking over at her with his piercing dark eyes as he pulled to a stoplight.

"About the kiss?" She gulped back the awkwardness, surprised he'd want to know.

"No," Tao chuckled, seeming to take pleasure in her squirming. "Are you going to tell him about what happened with Denver?"

Frankie's head had been swimming so much, worrying about her own future, she hadn't really given it much thought. She was shocked that her first instinct was no. "I don't think I will," she admitted.

"Why? Don't you trust him?" Frankie could read the nature of his question. *How can you even think to be with him if you couldn't trust him with this?*

"It's not that. It would be too out of context for him. He'd try to persuade me to write the story and break it all wide open. Somehow he'd have a thousand really valid points, and we'd argue. I don't want to do that. You and I made the right choice today. We did what was best for everyone, and I don't want to second guess that. Maxwell would have a hard time letting it go. It's better if I just keep it between us." Frankie didn't really like her answer. It didn't paint Maxwell in a good light, but ultimately it was true.

"So you have no story to tell," Tao stated flatly, staring at her even though the light was green now. "That's got to be hard for you. That whistle-blower website was prepared to get something from you. You had something that would exceed their expectations, and you let it go."

"It's just a setback." She shrugged. "I'll have a whole career full of great stories. I hope no matter what, I make choices that don't hurt people. That's not the kind of journalist I want to be. It's not the kind of person I want to be."

"You aren't," Tao insisted, finally pulling forward. "I promised I'd have your back, Frankie, no matter what you chose, and I am standing by that. I like you. I think that's pretty obvious by now. But don't let that put pressure on you. It's the last thing I'd want. You did the right thing today, even though it was hard. Now you should do what's right for you."

The rest of the ride back to the university was quiet, comfortably so. When she hopped out of the car and waved goodbye she felt like she'd slapped him in the face, even though he was insisting it was no big deal.

Settling back into the library, she stared down at her phone and waited patiently to hear from Maxwell. Their relationship deserved a chance, a conversation at least. She was sure of that now. He was still the Maxwell she'd dreamed about for the last few years. It wasn't possible for a bad week to change all that. Or at least that was what she kept telling herself.

Chapter Twenty-One

Maxwell leaned down and kissed her lips, and she could sense his remorse in it. He truly was sorry. The fear that his kiss would seem different this time evaporated. He was still the same Maxwell. He still smelled and felt exactly the same, and the butterflies still fluttered in her stomach.

"I'm really sorry," he said, his hands planted on her waist. "I feel like a jerk. I'm going to be busy, but I never want to be too busy for you."

He led her into the quiet Mexican restaurant and pulled out her chair. When he sat across from her he stared for a moment, smiling sweetly at her.

"I shouldn't have taken it so personally," Frankie admitted, waving off the apology rather than accepting it. "This is a big opportunity for you, and I was acting selfish, I guess." She wasn't sure where some of this was coming from. This wasn't what she'd been telling herself for days, but sitting here with him now was like sitting across from the rest of her life. Maybe she'd never love anyone again the way she loved him. Couldn't she power through a rough patch to make this work?

"The internship wasn't expected, especially somewhere so prestigious I'd have to work so hard right out of the gate. You had a plan when you got out here, and I just quit on you." He reached across the table and grabbed her hand.

"But what does that mean?" Frankie asked, tilting her head and looking at him curiously. "You wouldn't have dropped the internship to do my thing, right?"

"Well, no," Maxwell said with a chuckle. "You know this is setting up my career right now. I'd be crazy to be pulled away from that. But I could have done a better job talking to you. It was late, and I was tired, but I could have called to check in every night. Snuck away and sent you a couple text messages to let you know I was still alive."

Frankie nodded her head as though she agreed, but she wasn't exactly sure a couple more text messages would have made a difference.

"So tell me what happened with your dad," he said, turning his cell phone over so the flashing screen and constant chirping would stop.

"He's so pissed," she moaned, thinking about her father's angry words. "He got a call from the University of Arizona about my scholarship status, and he flipped that I had applied and not told him. I tried to explain we had a good plan, and we love each other, but he kept getting angrier. Finally he told me he'd ship all my stuff out here and not to come home." Her voice faltered under the weight of that. *Don't come home.*

"I'm sure he'll cool down, and it'll work out. But it's kind of a good thing, right?" Maxwell leaned in close, lowering his head so he could catch Frankie's downturned eyes. "Eventually he'll come around, they all will, but now we can get the apartment squared away and do what we were hoping. So when I'm crazy all day at the internship, you'll be there when I get home. We won't have to worry about late night text messages or anything. You'll be right there."

"That's true," she agreed, looking at him finally. The thoughts that had clouded her brain for the last year rolled back in. The idea of sharing an apartment with Maxwell and being together every night became clear in her mind again. But equally clear were Tao's words. Would she be just a toy on the shelf waiting for him every night?

"I've already looked at a couple places, and we could sign a lease as early as next week. Then shop for furniture and dishes and all that stuff. It'll be awesome. When your parents see how well we're doing, I know they'll come around. They can't stay mad at you, just like, hopefully, you can't stay mad at me." With the flash of his puppy-dog eyes he'd made his point.

"It sounds perfect," she replied, feeling like everything she wanted was dancing at her fingertips.

"Then let's do it. Come back over the weekend, and I'll carve out some time to go apartment hunting. Then even if we don't have a lot of time it'll be quality over quantity. Right?" His eyes were so hopeful she felt bad for having any hesitation.

"I have a couple things to take care of," she explained. "I want to finish what I started on the reservation, then I'll be able to think about this more clearly." Her words were the pin that popped his balloon of excitement. He didn't expect any type of hesitation on her part, and frankly why would he? In the past she'd jumped at every opportunity to be with him, talk to him, or even swap emails. This was the first reluctance she'd ever shown.

"I guess I'll have to live with that for now. I'll settle for a maybe because it's better than a no. Are you hungry?" He opened his menu and began skimming for what might be good.

"You're not mad I need more time?" she asked, reading his face and looking for any tiny clues of his real feelings.

"Frankie, you're worth waiting for."

Chapter Twenty-Two

The best Maxwell could do was pay to send her home in a cab. He couldn't spare the time to pick up the rental car his insurance company offered and drive her all the way back to the reservation himself. The cab ride gave Frankie lots of time to think but provided absolutely no clarity. When she crept to the front door of Shayna and Tao's house, she prayed he was asleep. She wasn't sure how she would answer when he asked how it went.

But when she pushed the door open she saw a welcomed surprise. "Shayna!" she shouted, dropping her bag and running to hug her friend. "I didn't think you were coming back this week."

"It was so boring there I couldn't take it anymore. I told my aunt if she didn't let me go home I'd start locking myself in my room. I was worried about you."

"I know; so much has been going on. I have no idea what I'm supposed to do." Frankie rubbed her forehead to work out the hammering pain that had started over dinner.

"I'm sorry I had to leave you with my brother; that must have been a nightmare." Shayna sat down on the couch and patted the spot next to her.

Frankie's eyes drifted to Tao's bedroom door before she spoke. "He wasn't bad at all. He helped me a lot."

"He's not here; you don't have to say that," Shayna snorted and rolled her eyes at the idea that her brother was helpful.

"Where is he?" Frankie asked, knowing he wasn't working and checking her watch, realizing how late it was.

"I don't know exactly. He went out for a while. He said he was going to be camping for a few days. He does that all the time." Shayna was positively buzzing with excitement, and she could tell that Frankie wasn't quite as thrilled. "What's the matter? Are you still pissed that your parents made you come here rather than being with Maxwell? That is super harsh. You finally thought you guys were going to get all serious, and boom, you end up in this hellhole."

Frankie shook her head, looking toward the front door and wondering if Tao had left because he knew she'd have worked things out with Maxwell. "No, it's not that. My parents told me to do what I want and not bother coming home."

"So what are you doing here? I would think you'd want to spend the night with Maxwell." Shayna was raking over her face now, positive something was up.

"It's a little complicated. I was spending a lot of time with Tao and . . ." Frankie wrung her hands nervously as she tried to get the story out. She and Shayna had spent so many hours traveling, bunking, and learning together that they might as well be sisters. Frankie was the first to find out when Shayna kissed a boy from the opposing debate team. Shayna knew every detail of Frankie's early feelings for Maxwell. Their bond was strong and woven together with a thousand personal details of teenage life.

"Shut up," Shayna shouted, shooting to her feet. "You fell for my stupid brother? No, this is not happening. Maxwell is the smartest and most driven guy I have ever met. As your best friend I will not allow you to throw that away for some stupid crush on my brother."

"It's not like that," Frankie lied and then gave in. "Fine, it's kind of like that, but I don't think it's just a crush. Tao has been so nice to me, and he is really insightful. Meanwhile Maxwell has been so focused on his own stuff that we've barely talked. He told me he would be busy, and I kept saying how fine I was with that. I'm not sure I'm fine with it at all. I don't know if that's what I want for my life. Now I have no idea what to do. I kissed Tao and . . ."

"In an effort to be a good friend right now I'm going to try to be objective and also not throw up. So you're telling me this isn't just a little passing thing with Tao, you actually have feelings for him?" Shayna sat back down and took her friend's hand in hers.

"Yes," Frankie admitted as she started to cry. "I never thought I'd have feelings for anyone but Maxwell. Tao is sweet, and he gets me in a way I'm not sure Maxwell ever has. I thought I was ready for this grown-up real life relationship with Maxwell, and now I'm not sure. I told him I'd let him know in a couple days if I'd go apartment shopping with him. I don't know what to do. My parents are pissed, Maxwell expects me to commit to our relationship, and I'm not ready to act like I don't feel anything for Tao. You have to help me figure this out."

Shayna sat with wide eyes as her normally very composed friend began falling apart. "I don't have a lot of advice, but I do believe one thing. I believe if you are in love with two people at the same time then you should let go of the first one. If you truly loved him you'd have been too preoccupied for anyone else to even get on your radar. If you made room for Tao in your life, then your feelings for Maxwell might not be what you thought they were."

Danielle Stewart

"That makes sense," Frankie said, wiping her stinging eyes. "But I can't imagine not being with Maxwell. My dad likes him, and that's a big deal. You know my dad really well; can you believe he told me not to come home? I didn't see that coming."

"Your dad probably felt like he was out of options. I'm sure you can work it out with them once they cool off. But before you do, you need to decide what you're fighting for. There's no point going back and arguing if you don't know what you want."

"I'm really glad you're back." Frankie laughed through her tears as she leaned in for a hug. "I knew you could smack some sense into me."

"Sure," Shayna smiled. "I kind of wish my brother wasn't in the equation, but I can see why you two would get along so well. You're a lot alike. You're both a pain in my ass."

"I also broke your shower," Frankie apologized. "And I wrecked Maxwell's car. It hasn't been a good week for me. But at the same time, it's been an incredible week."

"So what are you going to do while you make up your mind? You're welcome to stay here. Tao will be gone for a couple days. It'll be just me and you."

"There is something I want to do. I have an idea for an article I want to write, but I need some help. It's not quite what I had in mind when I got here, and maybe no one will ever read it. But it's important. Will you help me?"

"I'd love too. I've been playing with my little cousins for a couple weeks, and I swear my brain was turning to mush. Give me something important to do."

180

"So let's do it," Frankie said, pulling her computer out of her bag and flipping it open. She always did better when she had a goal.

"You never take a break, do you?" Shayna asked, looking at her friend with fake annoyance. "I'll pop some popcorn."

Chapter Twenty-Three

Shayna had come through for Frankie in a way she could never repay. Her friend was able to take a swirling mess of emotions and indecision and offer her support and love that distracted and calmed her. Coupled with the amazing help she'd given for Frankie's new endeavor of writing a different article, and she couldn't help but smile when thinking of Shayna.

Frankie had barely slept in days, and she'd flip-flopped a thousand times on what she should do. But yesterday morning she'd woken from a fitful sleep and had had her answer. It was right there in front of her the whole time. All she needed to do was act. So she did.

She'd finally arrived in the place she was meant to be. She could feel it. The answer was clear as she watched him across the way, her heart swelling with love. When she weighed out every mistake she'd made, every dream she'd had, and every risk she'd ever taken there was only one person she could see in her corner. She looked down at the paper copy of the article she'd written and couldn't wait to show it to him. It wasn't the most sensationalized or groundbreaking piece, but it was powerful. It was the best thing she'd ever written, and he'd like it. She glanced down and read the title out loud. *Cultural Sensitivity in Mental Health Treatment: A Native American's Journey of Healing the Mind.*

Danyia's story was one of many in the country, and the more Frankie read, the more she heard the same thing over and over again. Native Americans suffering from mental health issues were not seeking treatment because it either went against their beliefs, or they felt their cultural solutions were being dismissed too quickly. There was a need for a treatment plan that took both modern medicine and ancient beliefs into consideration. Some sensitivity and open mindedness was imperative.

Shayna had taken Frankie on a journey of understanding as they moved through challenges that faced a reservation. This was only one facet. Frankie could write an entire book on the injustice, conflict, and pain that still lingered all across the country for Native Americans. Frankie felt the spark of excitement burning in her belly as she thought of the voice she could give them. Hardly any of the reservations had their own media sources, which meant when there was something to say, there wasn't anywhere to say it. They needed a platform on which to speak. Maybe that would be something she would do someday. The possibilities seemed endless, and now she finally felt like her head was in the right place to get it done. Now all she needed was the guy to help her.

She could see him, but he couldn't see her. There was a part of her that wished she could make that last a while longer. Though she'd practiced what she would say dozens of times, she still worried it would come out wrong.

Finally, willing herself to do it already, she grabbed her bag out of the dirt and started walking toward him. All of her nerves evaporated when the look on his face told her everything she needed to know. He was happy to see her. He was relieved. He was excited. She opened her mouth to speak and watched his face crumple with emotion. She hadn't expected tears.

"Daddy," she whispered through a crackling voice. "I'm so, so—" her voice was cut short by his tight, suffocating hug.

"Frankie, I'm the one who's sorry. I tried the call you this morning, and I got your voicemail. I was wrong to tell you not to come home. You can always come home." He squeezed her so hard the air escaped her lungs, and she couldn't speak. But she didn't care; she wouldn't let go. She wouldn't let him let go.

"I'm sorry, I'm crushing you," he said, loosening up just a little as he wiped his eyes dry.

"Are you busy, Dad, or can we talk for a while?" Frankie asked as she looked at the house and noticed her mother's car wasn't there.

"I always have time for you. What did you have in mind?" he asked, his smile wider than she'd ever seen.

"How about one of those picnics we used to have when I was little?"

"I'll get the blanket, you get as much junk food as you can carry. Meet me under the tree in the backyard." They both headed into the house and went to work. She grabbed a basket and began filling it with chips and chocolate. Anything she could find that was unhealthy. Her mother didn't keep much in the house, but it would do for now.

A few minutes later they were sprawled out on the blanket, stuffing their faces, and laughing until their sides ached.

"I really didn't mean to hurt you and Mom when I left. I don't know what I was doing. That wasn't me, or not who I want to be anyway." The mood changed to a more serious one, and Michael sat up so he could see her better.

"Thanks. It's good to hear. I know you're trying to find your way, and you really do love Maxwell. It's hard, but we can find a way to make this work."

"I do love Maxwell," she replied. "I think I might love him the rest of my life, but I don't want to be with him. We're in two different places in our lives, and as much as this kills me to say, we're not together anymore."

Michael gripped the blanket tightly as though if he tugged the blanket his fragile daughter might blow away. "I'm so sorry that happened Frankie. But it sounds like you gave it a lot of thought."

"I did. When I was out there I spent a lot of time with Shayna's brother, Tao. He's my age and the complete opposite of Maxwell in most ways. I like him a lot." She could feel her cheeks warm as she explained this to her father.

"I see. So you're dating Tao now?" he asked, and she could tell how hard he was trying to move gently through this conversation.

"No," Frankie said shaking her head somberly. "I'm not dating Tao right now either. There's something I need to tell you, and I just want you to keep an open mind, please."

Michael drew in a deep breath as if he were stepping onto the moon. He nodded his agreement to her request but didn't speak.

"I know how important education is to you and Mom. It's really important to me too. I've spent four years showing you how much it meant to me and working my tail off to get into a good college."

"And apparently you got into at least two of them," Michael interjected, reminding her of her secret applications out of state.

"I'm not going to Arizona for school, Dad," she assured him, reaching across and touching his hand gingerly. "But I'm also not ready to start school here in North Carolina either."

"You've been accepted somewhere else?" he asked, fighting with his facial expressions to not look annoyed.

"No, well . . . I was accepted at a few other places, but I'm not going to them either. Not yet. That's what I wanted to tell you. I'd like to take a year off. I spent so much time trying to get into a school; I forgot to appreciate all I had here. I didn't treat my last year with you guys like it would be my last year."

"Well, it won't be." Michael laughed. "You're not going off to the electric chair; you're going to college. No matter which one you choose you'll be coming home to visit." He ran his hand over her hair the way he'd been doing for almost two decades.

"I know that, Dad, but I think you can admit that it won't be the same. Once I go, even when I visit, things will be different. But if I stay here one more year, I can work and get a chance to spend time with everyone without all the pressure of planning my future. I can make a decision about a school for the right reasons. This probably isn't your first choice for me, so I understand if we need to talk about it more."

"I think it deserves a bit more conversation. Maybe we get your mom's opinion on it too. Ultimately it'll be up to you to decide, and you know we want you here, so you don't have to worry about that. This will always be your home."

"I know that, Dad," Frankie felt every ounce of weight and stress that had piled on top of her since she left melt away. "I just need a chance to recharge and appreciate this place and my family."

"What about the article you were going to write; did that at least turn out well?" Michael asked, looking at the paper she had carried over with her.

"No," she said simply. "It didn't."

"You couldn't pull it together?" he asked, looking shocked at her out-of-character failure.

"Actually I helped find evidence of a seventeen-year-old conspiracy and tracked down a suspected murderer. Tao and I worked on it together, and he actually saved my butt when I wrecked Maxwell's car, and he thought this guy was responsible."

"You wrecked a car and were face to face with a murderer?" Michael looked like he might get sick.

"Not exactly," she said, rolling her eyes.

"Just promise when we tell this to your mom and grandmother we give them the sterilized version. So what did you do?"

"The story became much bigger than the one I went out there to research."

"But you didn't write it?"

"I couldn't. There were all sorts of people involved that would have suffered if I did. Good people who didn't deserve to go through that. I helped find a way to make it work for everyone. I just didn't write the story." She shrugged it off, but her father's expression was worth more than any accolades she would have received by writing it.

"That's my girl." He congratulated her on her choice. "And this Tao?" Michael asked, raising an eyebrow at her. "He saved the day? You don't plan to hop a train any time soon to go see him?"

"Not without telling you first." She smiled. "And I was actually going to ask you when Shayna came to visit next month, if Tao could come too. I'd like you to meet him."

"I think we can work something like that out," Michael grinned, reaching for a bag of chips and pulling it open. "I always knew I couldn't keep you little forever, but man, this really snuck up on me."

"Me too," Frankie joked lying flat on her back and staring up at the clouds the way they used to when she was little. He rolled next to her and tucked his arms behind his head.

"I wish we could stop time," Michael admitted.

"That's what I'm trying to do, I think, by staying home for a while. I want to take it all in. I'm tired of being too busy to go shopping with Mom or missing Ian's baseball games because I'm studying. I don't want to miss a single meal at Grammy's house. I know I'll have to do it someday, but maybe I can stop time for just a little while."

"Maybe." Michael sighed. "We all need a little of that I guess. This has been a rough patch."

"I picked you, Dad," she whispered. "I was sitting thinking about these two perfectly great guys and trying to plan my life around either of them and then I thought about all the things you've taught me. I deserve someone's full attention. I don't need to sacrifice everything that's important to me for a guy. I came home because I knew even if I had to walk away from two perfectly good men, I'd still have one waiting for me back here."

"You can always come home, Frankie. We'll be here for you. If you feel lost or alone, turn your compass toward this house, and we'll help you find your way.

Growing up isn't easy, we all have to do it, but you don't have to do it alone."

"Can we go pick Mom and Ian up?" Frankie asked, sitting up and clapping her hands together. "We need to get the fantastic four back together."

They both jumped to their feet and headed for Michael's car. "Thanks for forgiving me, Dad," Frankie said, wrapping her arms around his waist.

"Thanks for coming back and giving me a chance to." He kissed the crown of her red hair and, for a split second, she was five years old again, and his hair wasn't silver on the sides. The world was simple, and she had years left before she had to go anywhere. For just a fraction of a moment they were back to being just Daddy and daughter in the least complicated form. It was fleeting, blowing away on the wind that moved her hair and cooled her skin.

She wasn't five years old. Things weren't simple, but one thing hadn't changed. Family was still the solid foundation she could build her life on. Tonight when they all sat on the porch at her grandmother's house chatting about what she'd missed and how they were glad to have her back she'd take it all in. Nothing would distract her from the perfection right in front of her. And when the sun set she'd ask her grandmother for a bottle. She'd march herself out to the front yard with her cousin's and little brother and she wouldn't stop chasing fireflies until her bottle was glowing bright as a star. Because it wasn't about what ended up in the bottle, it was about how much fun you could have while you filled it up.

The End

189

Danielle Stewart

Note to the Reader:

To the loyal readers of the Piper Anderson Series and The Edenville Series.

I want to thank you all for visiting the town of Edenville and the characters that live in it over the years. We've travelled as far back as 1960 and followed the children now through adulthood. The most common message I receive every day is from readers wondering if I'll be continuing the series. They ask that I please keep the story going because they love to visit and stay connected to the characters. I reply personally to all these messages but wanted to address the question here as well. Edenville to me is like a vacation spot that I am lucky enough to visit frequently in my mind. I can't see a day where I won't be writing a book that takes us all back there. There are so many characters that we've met over the years that have stories to be told. There will be more books. I'll be writing different stories in different worlds along the way as well, and I hope you read those too. But I will visit Edenville for as long as I have characters there that have stories to tell. Betty has so much more to say and I don't intend to quiet her down any time soon.

Thank you for the kind reviews, the special notes you send me, and the continued support. You've given me the chance to make a career out of the one thing I truly love and I'll be forever grateful to you all for that.

Danielle Stewart

A Message from Betty

Hey pssst...

Yeah you there reading this book. It's me Betty. You know how I know what's best for everyone? Well then listen here. If you want to have a chance to win some money and be the first to know when more stories about me, and the rest of the gang come out then click the little doohickey below and sign up for the newsletter. You'll just get word about new releases. No junk. She'd be dumber than a bag of hammers to be bugging people so no need to worry about that. Now go on and take the two seconds that could get you some extra dough in your pocket. Well whatcha waiting for... Go on.

Visit www.authordaniellestewart.com

Sign up to be informed about the latest releases and get a free download of Midnight Magic – a novelette. Also, every month a newsletter subscriber will be randomly chosen to win a $25 egift card.

Danielle Stewart

Author Contact:
Website: AuthorDanielleStewart.com
Email: AuthorDanielleStewart@Gmail.com
Facebook: Author Danielle Stewart
Twitter: @DStewartAuthor

Books by Danielle Stewart

Piper Anderson Series
Book 1: Chasing Justice
Book 2: Cutting Ties
Book 3: Changing Fate
Book 4: Finding Freedom
Book 5: Settling Scores
Book 6: Battling Destiny

Piper Anderson Extras:
Chris & Sydney Collection – Choosing Christmas &
Saving Love
Betty's Journal - Bonus Material (suggested to be read
after Book 4 to avoid spoilers)

Edenville Series – A Piper Anderson Spin Off
Book 1: Flowers in the Snow
Book 2: Kiss in the Wind
Book 3: Stars in a Bottle

The Clover Series
Hearts of Clover - Novella & Book 2: (Half My Heart &
Change My Heart)
Book 3: All My Heart
Book 4: Facing Home

Midnight Magic Series
Amelia

Made in the USA
Middletown, DE
24 March 2016